Instinct told him so[...]
he'd learned a long t[...]
his gut, because those instincts were usually right.

They came to the end of the walkway, and as they stepped off the curb and onto the asphalt, the peal of three rapid gunshots ripped through the air, echoing like crackling thunder.

"No!" Paige screamed. Her shoulder bag hit the ground as she dropped for cover, crouching beside it, throwing her arms over her head.

Seth spun toward her, Glock raised. "Come on, let's get out of here." He grabbed Paige's hand, pulling her to run. They took off in a sprint, skirting around vehicles, his gaze swinging back and forth across the lot, trying to get a handle on where to go next.

More gunshots came from behind. Bullets whizzed past their heads.

"This way," Seth yelled and ducked right, pulling Paige with him. They rounded the corner just as another burst of gunshots lit the air like fireworks. Glass shattered, spitting jagged shards into the air in all directions.

"Seth! We're going to get killed!" Paige's panicked scream echoed above the explosive din.

Not if he could help it.

Annslee Urban grew up watching old-time romance movies, to which she attributes her passion for sweet romance, true love and happy endings. Raised in the foothills of Arizona, she survived temperature shock when she moved to western Pennsylvania, before settling in North Carolina with her husband and children. Aside from writing, Annslee enjoys cooking, traveling, playing with grandbabies and all things chocolate! You can reach Annslee at maryannsleeurban@gmail.com.

Books by Annslee Urban

Love Inspired Suspense

Smoky Mountain Investigation
Broken Silence
Deadly Setup

Visit the Author Profile page at Harlequin.com.

DEADLY SETUP

ANNSLEE URBAN

HARLEQUIN® LOVE INSPIRED® SUSPENSE

Recycling programs for this product may not exist in your area.

LOVE INSPIRED BOOKS

ISBN-13: 978-0-373-44775-6

Deadly Setup

www.Harlequin.com

Printed in U.S.A.

I can do all this through Him who gives me strength.
–Philippians 4:13

To my beautiful sisters in Christ: Nancy Lindsey, Sandi Mashburn and Barbara Cohn.
Angels are often sent as friends. Blessings to you, my friends!

And to my grandkiddos: Cameron, Kaylee, Adelyn, Isaac, Ainsley and Jayce. I love you to the moon and back.

ONE

Am I being followed?

The thought circled through Paige Becker's brain and sent her pulse skittering. She darted a glance in the rearview mirror, squinting against the rain-pelted windshield. The fall storm had picked up, making visibility almost impossible. But behind her, in the distance, the low white glow of headlights burned up the fog and darkness as a vehicle came careening around a bend in the road.

Suddenly Paige was frightened. A pickup had been riding her bumper down Highway 321 in Boone, North Carolina. She'd breathed relief when the light turned red as the driver pulled off at the exit behind her, forcing him to stop. Had the same mysterious vehicle caught up with her?

Lightning flashed, and a burst of thunder shook the Jeep. Paige jumped, and for a moment she lost control of the vehicle. The rear of the Renegade started to skid, fishtailing on the rain-slicked asphalt toward the shoulder of the road. Toward the steep bank.

Panic rioted through Paige's chest. She yanked the steering wheel to the left, muscles clenching, and managed to steer the Jeep away from the edge and back into her lane.

Thank You, Lord.

Chest heaving, she worked to catch her breath. Bright lights reflected in her side-view mirrors. The truck had caught up with her and was back on her bumper. An empty, nauseated feeling erupted in the depths of her stomach.

Was this a case of road rage? Or had her return to Boone incensed someone, fearful of what evidence she might dig up?

A chill needled her bones. *Okay.* She yanked her handbag from the seat beside her and riffled for her cell phone. It was time to call the police.

Fear. Anger. Frustration. A tangled mess of emotions churned in her gut when her search came up empty. As she tossed her bag on the seat beside her, she spied a small blinking light on the floor by the passenger door. Her cell phone.

On a sigh, she dug her nails into the wheel and glanced at the steep winding curves ahead of her. *Oh, no.* She darted a look between the road ahead and the rearview mirror. The truck was still there. The rain had eased up a little, allowing just enough light for her to make out a silhouette of a man inside the cab. *Is this lunatic planning to run me off the road?*

Before the frantic thought fully penetrated her brain, the roar of an engine hit her ears, and the driver barreled into the lane beside her.

Heart thumping, Paige nailed the accelerator to the floor and held her breath, praying her car wouldn't lose traction again. If she could only make it a couple more miles, she'd be in view of a gas station and well-lit shopping area. *Please, Lord.*

But instead the truck matched her speed, edging to the right, encroaching into her lane.

Sweat slickened Paige's palms as she clenched the wheel and veered right, precariously hugging the edge of the pavement. Her Jeep was now halfway up the steep incline and beginning the curve. She just needed to get over the hill. Just one more mile.

Her faint glow of hope extinguished a split second later as the truck swerved sharply and slammed into her door, sending her vehicle hurtling off the roadway and back onto the shoulder.

No! She gritted her teeth, trying to gain control. Brakes whined and tires spun, churning up mud and gravel.

Thunder rumbled and growled. Rain came down in sheets.

Sucking in a sharp breath, Paige jerked the wheel to the left, bringing the vehicle bouncing back onto the asphalt. But instead of gaining control, the Jeep started to hydroplane. With brakes squealing and tires screeching, the Renegade skidded like a pendulum from one side of the road to the other.

Fear sent crushed ice through her veins as the Jeep's back end struck a tree just before sailing over the edge of the embankment. It rolled several times before finally coming to a dead halt. Paige's head hit the steering wheel, and the air bag deployed on impact.

Everything went dark.

Deputy Detective Seth Garrison turned his headlights to high beam and accelerated down the long stretch of highway. He'd finally made it back to Boone. In another fifteen minutes, he'd be home, kicking off his boots and plopping down in his old leather recliner. After a week away in Raleigh painting and making repairs on his mom's house, he was ready for a little R & R.

Around a tight bend in the road and in the distance, flashing lights burned up the night fog. Red. Blue. White. Watauga County rescue vehicles.

Welcome home. Seth released a long breath. Not even ten miles into the county and work was there to greet him. So much for that R & R.

Seth arrived at the scene. Fire, police and rescue vehicles were scattered across the two-lane highway, their blinking lights reflecting off the icy road. He pulled his hat on and grabbed his jacket and a flashlight. There was a damp chill in the air as temperatures continued to drop. All around him residual puddles from the earlier storm had started to freeze.

Ice creaked and splintered beneath his boots as he hiked up a slight incline and navigated his way to a small company of police and rescue workers congregated at the edge of the embankment.

Before he could ask, Officer Ted Hanson swung his grim face toward him. "We've got a car in the ravine. A local resident on his way home saw the vehicle spin out and slide off the road."

"Casualties?" Seth swept his flashlight around the wooded area at the bottom of the ditch, stopping when his light caught on the Jeep resting in a thicket of small pines and scrub. The roof of the vehicle had been sliced off. The rescuers had put the Jaws of Life into action, and now four firefighters were working the scene.

"Amazingly, no." Ted stuffed his hands in the pockets of his police-issue bomber jacket. "Single driver. A woman. EMS radioed up a few moments ago to say she had come to and her injuries didn't appear life threatening, but no update on her identity."

"She's fortunate, whoever she is."

"We're coming up," one of the rescuers announced over the radio in a scratchy voice, almost lost in the static.

Ten minutes later two firefighter paramedics emerged from the scene with the victim strapped on a backboard. Other rescue workers rushed over and helped get her on a gurney.

Battery-powered floodlights lit up the scene. The woman was in full spinal precautions. A trail of crimson trickled down one cheek from a gash on her forehead, and long strands of her dark curls spilled over the edge of the wooden backboard. She was shaking uncontrollably, her teeth chattering, her breathing unsteady.

Everything inside Seth froze as his heart slammed to a disturbing halt. He knew that face.

Paige Becker.

Automatically, he took a step, then stopped, summoning every ounce of control he could muster, and still he had to force himself not to go to her. He would be the last person she would want to see right now.

What was Paige doing back in Boone?

As a trio of emergency workers maneuvered the gurney over the ice-slicked roadway, a firefighter called out, "We're going to need warm blankets."

"Ready and waiting." A medic jumped out of the back of the EMS vehicle and helped load up the victim.

"Is that…Paige Becker?" Ted cut Seth a sideways glance. "I didn't know she was back in town."

Seth didn't respond. The bile scalding his throat wouldn't let him. Rough breakups never healed easy. He pushed his hat up on his forehead and fought to shove old feelings aside as he watched the doors to the EMS vehicle slam shut.

Be okay, Paige. Those three little words played in his head.

She had to be. She was the most resilient woman he knew.

Paige woke up in a dimly lit room, a hammer pounding inside her head, her mind fuzzy. She gingerly shifted against the unfamiliar bed. Every bone in her body hurt.

As she looked around the small area, thoughts and memories untangled in her mind. It took a few moments for her to remember where she was and why.

"Boone Memorial," she muttered as the jumbled bits and pieces of the night started to meld together. She'd been in an accident. Her Jeep had run off the side of the road.

Suddenly, as if a veil of brain fog lifted, every detail came rushing back with startling clarity. *No.* Paige jerked up straight in the bed. *Someone ran me off the road.*

The room started to spin. Vision blurred. Paige swayed and then gripped the metal railing. She pulled in a breath against the assailing head rush and lowered herself against the raised angle of the bed. She blew it out slowly, letting the dizziness pass.

She was reeling from exhaustion and whatever medication she'd been given. She felt rotten. And to make matters worse, someone had tried to kill her. She'd like to chalk it up to a road-rage lunatic, but her gut told her different.

Fresh tears gathered, washing hot. Paige squeezed her eyes shut and swallowed hard. She'd only been in town since that morning, and already the message was clear: she wasn't welcome back in Boone. Someone didn't want her to find the truth. A chill prickled her flesh. She shook it off. She couldn't let fear paralyze her investigation. Her brother's life depended on her.

Voices drifted in from the hallway. She opened her eyes, realizing she was no longer alone. The door was cracked open, and she caught a glimpse of a nurse standing outside the room talking to someone. A pager went off. Loud and insistent, growing to an unforgiving wail.

Paige's headache burst to full bloom. Cringing, she pressed two fingertips to her pounding temple and rubbed vigorously. She mouthed *thank you* when the nurse silenced the device.

"If you'll excuse me, Detective, I have another patient to check on. Feel free to look in on Miss Becker, but remember, she's feeling rather rough from the accident and may not be up to many questions."

"Thank you. I shouldn't be long. I only need a short statement from her on what happened tonight."

The masculine voice ripped through the air like a bolt of lightning. Everything inside Paige went still. *Seth Garrison.* As if running off the side of a mountain wasn't bad enough. She rubbed her temple harder. What was he doing here?

Common sense kicked in, reminding her Seth was a detective for the sheriff's department. He was here to do his job.

A fresh spurt of annoyance bottled in her chest. His *job*—the sole reason her relationship with him—imploded. A man who went above and beyond the call of duty—even when he was wrong.

The door slowly creaked open.

Fighting a groan, Paige pulled herself into a sitting position. She pushed strands of hair from her face, licked her lips. She kept her expression placid, nonchalant. Hopefully, she looked somewhat together.

Just stay strong, keep your head on straight, emotions intact.

That plan derailed about ten seconds after Seth's broad shoulders filled the doorway. Waves of hot and cold shuddered through her as she regarded him, fending off emotions that were far from intact. Feelings she thought she'd buried ten months ago when he'd ignored her pleas for justice, shattering her trust and her heart.

For a moment, Seth stood there, taking in the room, jaw set, legs planted slightly apart, arms at his sides. *A cop stance.* Even without a uniform, Seth was a cop to his core. His wide eyes, thickly lashed, under dark brows only further enhanced his stoic demeanor.

Tension coiled around her chest, squeezing tight as Seth stepped forward and stopped a foot from her bed. She looked up to see him, head cocked, eyes intent. She swallowed as they went soft and deep as he looked at her, the same dark gaze that still haunted her dreams.

Paige's heart froze as a bittersweet pang surged through her, stirring up memories of heartbreak and pain. Memories of Seth were always tough. Memories of the night he arrested her brother, Trey, and charged him with the brutal murder of his estranged wife, harder still.

Fresh anger ignited deep in her chest. Her brother was about to stand trial, facing a life sentence without parole. And the one man who could have helped track down the real killer halted the investigation and declared Trey Becker the only suspect.

"Paige, how are you feeling?"

She tried not to look at him. *Frustrated and disappointed* came to mind. She bit back a snide comment and forced herself to breathe. They'd been down that road too many times. "I've been better, Detective Garrison."

Her voice quivered. She swallowed tightly. So much for being strong.

Although it didn't help that after all the disappointment, all the pain, all it took was one look at Seth's strong, chiseled face and broad-shouldered physique and her traitorous stomach reacted with an inappropriate adolescent twist.

"The nurse told me the CT scan came out good. No broken bones," Seth said, his deep baritone resonating concern. She bit her lip, hard. Where was that concern ten months ago? When she really needed it, needed him? "You're fortunate," he continued. "You drove off one of the deadliest curves on the mountain pass and tumbled about fifty feet."

Her heart kicked at the reminder. *Thank You, Lord, for keeping me safe.* She looked up and blinked against Seth's assessing stare. "I'd like to clarify something, Detective. I didn't drive off the mountain. I was run off the road by another vehicle."

"Run off the road?" Seth's eyebrows climbed. "We received a report from a man on his way home that he saw a vehicle skid out of control before going off the road."

Paige took a shaky breath as pressure built in her chest just thinking about the horrible series of events. "The report you received was only partially correct. What the witness obviously didn't see was the truck that had been on my tail for miles down Highway 321. He'd followed me off the Eagle's Ridge exit. And before I could get away from him, he rammed into the side of my Jeep, sending me skidding out of control and into the ravine."

"What kind of truck?" Seth pulled a small pad from his pocket.

"Long bed, extended cab," she said, fingering her

necklace, still not believing what had happened. "It was dark and stormy. I couldn't make out much else."

Frown lines swept across Seth's forehead, narrowing his eyes. "And you didn't call the sheriff's office?"

His question cut to the core. *Sheriff.* After living through her brother's fiasco for the last ten months, Boone law enforcement wasn't exactly at the top of her list of people she hoped to run into during her return, *especially* Detective Seth Garrison.

Paige fought off a sigh and shrugged. "By the time I realized what was happening, I couldn't get to my cell phone and there was no safe place to pull over."

Seth looked as if he was going to say something but stopped. He probably wanted to chastise her for not being more careful. The former navy SEAL lived and breathed extreme caution. *Always keep your phone close and don't wait until something goes wrong. If you feel uncomfortable in a situation, get out of there and call for help.* His notorious words rang in her head. But instead of issuing a reminder, Seth straightened his broad shoulders. Full-on cop mode. Reminding her this wasn't personal. This was business.

She should have felt relief, but instead her heart slipped a bit.

"You mentioned the stormy weather conditions at the time of the accident," Seth said, jolting her back to the present.

Paige blinked and breathed deep, readjusting her focus to the accident and not the man asking the questions. She lifted her chin slightly. "Yes, the weather was terrible."

He raised a curious brow. "Is it safe to assume that you were traveling below the speed limit?"

"Yes." She shrugged one shoulder. "That is, until the

truck pulled up beside me, then I sped up trying to get away from him."

Seth gave a subtle nod and scribbled something on his notepad. Uneasiness prickled the fine hairs on the back of her neck. She could almost see the thoughts churning in his head, and she didn't like the vibes she was getting.

"Okay." Seth stuffed the notepad in his pocket and cast her a look that said, *I've got this figured out.* "It sounds to me like you were a victim to a hit-and-run. Impatient drivers often tailgate slower vehicles, and unfortunately stormy weather doesn't deter everyone. If the driver of the truck got annoyed and tried to get around you, his tires may have slipped on the wet road, which could have sent him into your lane."

Paige bristled at Seth's presumptuous assessment. He obviously wasn't listening. "No, that's not what happened," she snapped and struggled to sit up straighter. "The driver knew exactly what he was doing. He rammed into the side of my Jeep, and as I futilely fought to get my vehicle under control, he took off, vanishing into the night."

Seth looked back at his notes as if to process what she'd just said. The grim silence that followed did nothing to quell the anxiety churning inside her. "Paige—" He looked up at her, keeping his voice low, as if to de-escalate the situation. Like it was that easy. "Roughly 10 percent of all traffic accidents are hit-and-runs. And just as you described, they often involve an aggressive driver who causes the accident, then gets scared and takes off without stopping to help. Who knows, maybe this driver was even intoxicated."

Seth's simplistic cop logic sent adrenaline shooting through her veins. Some maniac had tried to kill her. Didn't he get that? Paige felt her jaw go rock hard as she tried to control the frustration exploding in her chest. "What this driver did was intentional, not an accident."

Seth perched a hand on the footboard and studied her, a question mark on his face. "Paige, is there a reason that you'd think someone would want to hurt you?"

Paige shivered as a montage of memories roared through her head. Spiraling, reeling, flooding her brain with such veracity she felt dizzy again. Madison's death. Her brother's arrest. Evidence and more evidence. The bloody knife. The DNA. The upcoming trial…a killer still on the loose.

She opened her mouth, barely getting the words out. "Yes, I do believe there's a reason someone would want to hurt me."

Seth's deep brown gaze locked on hers, probing, assessing. "And why is that?"

Her throat knotted. She lifted her chin. "Because, Detective, I came back to Boone looking for the truth."

Seth's brows rose again. *Truth?* No amount of evidence would ever be enough for this woman.

And the last thing he needed was Trey Becker's sister running around Boone, asking questions and stirring up more anger and strife toward her brother.

Seth felt a tight curl of frustration in his gut. Trey had been charged in the stabbing death of his estranged wife, Madison Cramer Becker. A death that sparked outrage in the community and left Boone residents with a bad taste in their mouths when it came to Trey Becker.

Even ten months later, that anger was still burning strong.

The Cramers were well-known, longtime residents in Boone. The family owned the local antique mart, and several generations still lived in the area.

A tight-knit bunch, but unfortunately not immune to tragedy. Ten years earlier, Frank Cramer, Madison's father, was killed after being involved in an accident with a drunk driver. His death spurred an outpouring of community support and sympathy for the surviving family members—Madison, her brother and her mother.

Many of those same residents now counted the days until Trey Becker's trial. They weren't going to rest until Madison's killer was convicted and facing life in prison without parole.

Paige couldn't have picked a worse time to come back.

"Paige, don't do this to yourself," Seth urged, knowing he was probably wasting his breath. "Trey has a good legal team on his case. Let them do their job."

"Are you kidding?" Paige shot him a look. "For ten months I sat back and let everyone 'do their job.'" Her fingers made air quotes. "Detectives, police, reporters, attorneys."

"And there's some strong evidence against Trey." Seth sighed, already growing annoyed by the conversation. "People have been doing their job."

"Really?" She let out a heavy sigh. "Then whose job is it to find evidence in support of my brother? Nobody seems to be doing that."

Seth took a deep breath, frustration battling with empathy. It wasn't like he hadn't given her brother the benefit of the doubt. Trey had been a friend. A fellow SEAL. But from the get-go, things hadn't looked good. When Seth and other officers arrived at Madison's home, they'd found Trey, his hands covered in blood. More blood on his clothes.

Forensics later confirmed Madison had been stabbed multiple times and her throat slit by a government-issue US Navy Ka-Bar, the combat knife presented to SEALs upon graduation. Evidence of Trey's fingerprints on the weapon and DNA at the scene hammered the final nail in his case.

Still, part of Seth got what Paige was doing. Trey was the only family she had left. Family was important. She wanted no stone left unturned. But, up to now, every stone they touched produced more evidence against her brother.

Seth spread his hands. "Paige, you know if new evidence turns up against anyone else, we'd reopen your brother's investigation. But right now, every shred of evidence we've come up with points to Trey."

A tousled, silky lock of hair tumbled in front of her face as Paige looked up, her eyes weary and pained, void of the tenacious glint that belonged to the woman he'd once loved. Grief stabbed him in the chest at her pain. And the worst part—there was nothing he could do to help.

"Come on, Seth." She gave a hard sigh, tucking the strand behind her ear. "It shouldn't surprise anyone that Trey's fingerprints and DNA were at the scene. He found Madison. And, as far as the knife goes, well, we both know evidence can be planted."

Seth nodded, absently drumming his fingers against his jeans-clad thigh. She wasn't saying anything he hadn't heard before. But it was hard to give much weight to Paige's deduction that Trey, who had been highly intoxicated the night of the murder, had been framed by the real killer. A theory that she hadn't budged from since her brother's arrest. And one that was a bit much for him to swallow.

"The truth is, Seth, Trey got caught in the crosshairs of your investigation and you never looked further." Paige continued, her eyes wide before she looked away in disgust, "You never even took into account that he tried to revive Madison and called the police."

A murder suspect calling police wasn't that unusual, Seth thought with a mental groan. Especially an intoxicated one. Alcohol, anger and impulsiveness were a lethal combination. He knew that from experience, growing up with an alcoholic father—a calm, sensible man until he was drinking. His family never knew what to expect. Seth had almost breathed relief at fourteen when his father stomped out of the house, suitcase in hand, screaming at the top of his lungs that he'd never be back.

That was the last time he'd seen his father and the last time he'd prayed. He'd learned how futile it was to pray for someone to change.

Seth put his hands on his hips. "Paige, I'm sorry for what you're going through. I know this ordeal has been difficult for you."

"Sorry?" Paige whipped her gaze back to him, her eyes sizzling. "The only thing you should be sorry about is that my brother is facing a life sentence in prison while a brutal killer is still running free."

"Paige—" When Seth tried to interject, she cut him off.

"Don't try to dispute it, Seth." She crossed her arms. "Trey would never hurt anyone, much less murder his wife. Even if he and Madison never worked out their issues, he still loved her."

Crimes of passion were impulsive acts. Add in alcohol or any mind-altering substance, and judgment could become impaired. And when someone was under the influence, it was even easier to lose self-control in the heat of the moment. "Gut feelings aren't enough, Paige."

"Then what about what happened tonight?" Her eyes

probed his face as she jutted her thumb back at herself. "Someone tried to kill me."

Seth folded his arms, frustration reigning supreme. "Paige, tonight's accident will be thoroughly investigated, however it's too early to assume anything."

"I know I'm only speculating," Paige said, her gown rustling as she straightened. "However, *if* tonight's accident was intentional, the only person I can think of with a motive to hurt me would be Madison's killer."

Seth started to shake his head, but Paige stopped him again with a staying hand. "Seth, it makes perfect sense. If my brother is convicted, the real killer gets off scot-free. The last thing the creep would want is for me to come back to town and start asking questions."

Good hypothesis—that was, if Seth thought Madison's killer was still out there. But, as the investigator on Paige's case, he'd hear her out. He tightened his arms over his chest. "Okay, Paige. Who knew you'd be in town today?" He asked the question, even though it struck at his heart that she hadn't even bothered to contact him.

"It was a last-minute trip. I only contacted my friend Tessa Riley." Even as she kept her expression placid, red crept into her cheeks. She'd caught his vibe. And he knew an excuse when he heard one. "I called Tessa yesterday after my boss at the rehab center gave me the time off to come. We're short staffed, but she knows about Trey's situation and how difficult it's been on me. However…" She sat up straighter. "After I arrived and dropped my bags off at Tessa's, I went out to do some errands and ran into several old friends and acquaintances."

Seth scratched his cheek. "Did anyone act suspicious?"

She thought a moment, then shook her head. "Everyone kept their distance. No one wanted to talk about Madison or discuss her murder. Although that's probably not unusual. However—" Paige emphasized the word "—the way news travels around here, half of Boone probably knows I'm in town by now."

True, but... Seth drew in a deep breath. It still sounded like a TV crime drama to him. Not to mention the theory was difficult to substantiate, given the information they had. "Paige, we've exhausted every lead we received on Madison's case. As much as I'd like to find something that would exonerate your brother, that just hasn't happened."

Paige grabbed the side rail, pulling herself up straighter in the bed. "That, Detective, is what I'm here to do."

Like rubbing salt in a wound. "Do what, Paige? Try to convince yourself that Trey just might be guilty?" Seth's tone was meant to be frank, but his frustration rang clearly.

One of Paige's brows soared upward, but she didn't respond. Just stared back at him, a steady, indignant look in her deep emerald eyes.

Instant regret knifed through him, not only for his blunt choice of words, but for everything that had gone wrong in their relationship. He'd made a vow early in his career to keep his personal life and detective work separate, but he should have worked harder to support Paige. Maybe then their relationship could have weathered this storm.

The heavy rock in his gut swelled to a boulder, telling him probably not.

He'd learned years ago that when someone was ready to bolt, there was no holding on to them. And after Trey's trial was moved to Durham County because of all the negative pretrial publicity, there was no holding Paige back. She had nothing left in Boone.

Including him.

Seth shifted his stance, ignoring the sting of heartache in his chest. "Paige, there's a lot of pent-up anger around this town. Coming back now and asking questions, especially on the brink of Trey's trial, isn't going to be easy on you."

Paige's mouth flattened to a thin line. "Sitting in a six-by-eight jail cell hasn't been easy on my brother, either."

Tension hung in the air, heavy and mounting. They were getting nowhere.

Scrubbing a hand through his hair, Seth mentally tamped down his feelings, frustrated by the sudden whiplash of emotions and memories. Emotion that had no place on the job.

Job. The reason he was there. He forced his focus back to the problem at hand—Paige's accident. He took a deep breath and zipped up his jacket. Time to get out of there. He had everything he needed. "Paige, will you be staying with Tessa while you're in town?"

Paige hesitated, her scowl remaining. "I'll be staying at her condo. She's out of town on a cruise for the next week."

Seth made a mental note and stuffed his hands in his coat pockets. "Get some rest. I'll touch base with you sometime tomorrow," he said, then turned and headed out the door, focusing his thoughts on his investigation and stowing all sentimental nonsense that had nothing to do with this case.

TWO

The next morning, Seth slumped into the swivel desk chair in his office at the Watauga County Sheriff's Department and picked up the police report detailing Paige's accident. He flipped through it, stopping at the picture of her mangled car.

Broken glass, deployed air bags, twisted metal.

How could anyone survive something like that? He dropped the report on his desk, rocked back in his chair and scrubbed his face. The thick foliage and spruce trees had cushioned the impact, but still.

He shook his head.

If he were a man of faith, he would definitely say someone up there had been looking out for her. For Paige to walk away from a crash like that with only a few bumps and bruises was hard to comprehend.

One thing he did comprehend, though, was that somebody had run her off the road. And that person hadn't bothered to stop. Or even call for help. Purposeful or not, that tidbit hit him deep in the gut. And his only clue so far was that *somebody* was driving a long-bed extended-cab pickup. Which narrowed the suspect list to about two-thirds of Boone's population.

Meaning—he had nothing.

Frustration banged around in his chest. He rocked forward in his chair and stood. He needed coffee.

In the break room, Seth grabbed the glass pot and poured himself a cup. Strong and black. Something to jump-start his brain. Right now every synapse in his head was seriously misfiring.

Seth took a sip of the steamy brew as he thought about how many hit-and-run accidents were never solved. A fact he hated to accept.

"Seth, what are you doing here?" Detective Colton Walsh said, walking into the room. "I thought you were still out of town."

In some respects he wished he still was. Seth leaned against the cabinet, sipping his coffee. "I got back yesterday. I had the rest of the week off and had plans to get some things done around my place, but I got pulled into a case last night."

"Last night?" Colton picked up the coffeepot, tilting it over an empty mug.

"The accident on Eagle's Ridge. I saw the flashing lights at the scene as I was heading home, and I just couldn't help myself," he admitted with a tight grin.

Pausing the pot midway, Colton glanced up, creasing his forehead. "I thought Brett Ralston was on that case. I think he just left to talk to the victim."

"What?" Seth snorted, almost choking on the sip he just took. "Ralston?"

Colton nodded. "The chief assigned him to the case this morning."

This day just kept getting worse. Seth pitched his cup and slammed out of the room. He headed down the long corridor to the office at the far end—the office of the Watauga County chief of detectives.

Seth's old friend Detective Kevin Mullins looked up

as he stalked into the room. "Kevin, could you please explain why you assigned Ralston to my case?"

Dropping his ink pen, the chief leaned back in his chair, steepling his fingers together, as if sizing up Seth's vehemence. "You're officially on vacation, Seth. I wasn't even sure if you'd be in today."

"I was up half the night writing up the accident report and the victim's statement, and it didn't cross your mind to pick up the phone and call me before you handed my case to someone else?"

The chief hesitated a moment and then swerved his chair around, getting to his feet. "Seth, I didn't want to have to tell you this, but Paige requested another detective be put on her case."

Seth looked Mullins in the eye. "You're kidding."

"No," Mullins said with a casual hitch of his shoulders. "It's not an unreasonable request. You're the detective responsible for her brother's arrest *and* she is your ex-girlfriend."

Irrelevant from Seth's perspective. His jaw clenched in exasperation. It was his case, and no one would do a better job investigating Paige's accident than him. Especially not Brett Ralston. He'd been a friend of Trey's, but like the rest of local law enforcement, he'd seen the evidence and believed Trey was guilty. Like that wasn't a conflict of interest for her, too.

"Seth, I'm sorry."

Seth didn't comment. Didn't protest. If Paige didn't want him on her case, fine.

Mullins studied him, eyes narrowed. "Are you going to be okay with this?"

Like he had a choice. Seth lifted a shoulder. "Sure. Absolutely."

"Good to hear." Mullins's face brightened. "Because

we've been drowning around here since you've been gone. Now that you're back, I have some things I'd like for you to get started—"

"Hold on, Chief." Seth waved a staying hand. "You were right when you said I'm still on vacation. And for the next week I plan to stay away from the office and out of sheriff's department business." He never should have stopped last night.

"But—"

"See you later, Chief." Seth lifted his hand in a saucy salute and turned to walk out of the office. Now more than ever he needed time off. To unwind, get some work done and hopefully forget about Paige.

Paige walked down the sidewalk toward Boone Auto Body and Wrecker, trying to keep pace with Deputy Detective Brett Ralston of the Watauga County Sheriff's Department. After a restful night, she was feeling the effects from her accident. Her limbs were stiff, body achy. But she wasn't complaining. At least she was out of the hospital. A couple ibuprofen and she'd be fine.

Instinctively, she reached for her shoulder bag, then realized it wasn't there. Her heart sank, reality settling in. Her purse and other personal things had been left inside her car. She drew in a deep breath and exhaled. Hopefully, her items had been recovered by the wrecker service.

Boone Auto Body and Wrecker was an older establishment that had been in business for decades. She entered the ancient brick building through a set of dingy glass doors and into a small waiting area. Everything around her was well worn, from the weathered wood reception desk to the cracked orange-vinyl chairs. The smell of grease and oil seasoned the air.

She blinked as tears bit her eyes. This was the final resting place for her spunky little Jeep, her first purchase after she graduated from college.

No big deal, she told herself. It was only a car. Still, she couldn't hold in a weary sigh.

"Are you okay?" Brett raised his bushy brows beneath his combed-back blond hair.

Okay was a relative term. She bit her lower lip. Leaning against one of the weathered wood pillars, she managed a nod.

A short, pudgy woman came around the corner carrying a cardboard box. "Miss Becker, here are the things recovered from your car."

Paige riffled through the menagerie of items. She hadn't realized how much stuff she'd crammed into her handbag, which had obviously erupted like a volcano on impact. Besides her wallet, most items in her purse were trivial—receipts, candy, pens, markers, even a few stray tubes of lip gloss. Several other items from her car were in the box as well—an umbrella, her Bible and a small satchel of paperwork, even her ring of keys. But where was her—

"Is that everything, Paige?"

Paige snapped her head up at Brett's question. "My phone. It's missing."

They both turned to look at the young woman behind the front desk, her name tag reading Lisa.

"Everything was removed from the car," Lisa said. "The wrecker brought it in early this morning and everything left of it has been stripped. The seats, carpet, even the dash is gone."

"Gone?"

"Anything that can be salvaged is taken out. Then everything else goes to scrap. You're fortunate we found what we did."

Paige's heart sank. The one thing she needed was gone.

"It shouldn't be too hard to get a replacement phone," Brett said.

Except her notes and the numbers for friends and family of Madison's that she wanted to contact were on that phone.

"Please sign this form, acknowledging receipt of your belongings," Lisa said, handing her a clipboard.

Paige scribbled her name on the line marked with an *X*, then started gathering her things, stuffing them back in her bag. Memories flashed in her head, errant bits and pieces of the night before—the storm, the truck, her Jeep tumbling down into the ravine. Just as quickly her thoughts switched to her brother, locked behind bars for a crime he'd never commit. Her mind fixed on that reality.

She wasn't going to let the loss of her vehicle or a cell phone stop her from uncovering the truth. Lord willing.

Later that day, sometime after three, she walked out of the phone store, her new cell phone tucked in her purse. She stepped through the arched portals of the Blue Ridge Marketplace, an outdoor shopping area of home-style restaurants and retail shops.

The anxiety-ridden adrenaline of the last twenty-four hours finally started to subside. Paige drew in a deep breath and let it out as she worked on getting her thoughts in order.

Ever since she could remember, her brother had been her protector. Their single mom took off when they were young, and although they were left in their grandmother's care, it was Trey who watched over her. Growing up, he made sure she had what she needed and never wanted her to worry about anything.

Even now with his freedom hanging in the balance, he wanted to protect her, which was why he'd tried to distance her from his case.

Paige, I don't want you to put your life and career on hold for me. Trey's oft repeated words rang in her head. She was twenty-eight, not a little girl anymore, and a counselor. Caring for others was her job. And who better to care for her brother?

Despite her brother's attempt to shield her from his troubles, she refused to sit by any longer. After months of constant badgering, Trey finally broke during her last visit with him and answered questions about Madison, her friends and family.

Although Trey and Madison had been married nearly a year, Paige never really knew her sister-in-law well. Madison stayed somewhat elusive when it came to Trey's family and friends. In fact she quickly pulled Trey into her world. A world built around her mother, brother and the family business.

Paige couldn't stop the surge in her heartbeat when she thought about how distant her brother had become after he got involved with Madison. If it hadn't been for Seth's love and support—

Whoa! Enough. Paige stomped down those thoughts and hurried along the sidewalk. She had a job to do and no time to waste wallowing in the past. Tomorrow would be here before she knew it, and she had more important things to think about than Seth—like figuring out who'd killed Madison.

She entered the parking deck and traversed the enclosed flight of switchback stairs that led to the fifth floor, where her rental car was parked. Two years earlier, city officials granted approval for this midtown shopping complex to be built. After months of delays, construction finally began just about the time she was leaving.

So much had changed in the ten months she'd been gone. Her picturesque little mountain town was moving up in the world.

Without her.

A wave of sadness swelled inside her. Paige shook it away and continued up the narrow stairs. As she approached the third-floor landing, her feet faltered, stopped cold by a thunderous metallic clank, which reverberated from several floors below her.

Paige grabbed the handrail.

A moment later, heavy footfalls sounded, reining in her panic. She heaved a silent sigh of relief. *A door slamming.* It was just someone heading to their car.

Stop being so edgy, she ordered herself.

Yesterday's storm and all the chaos that followed still had her on edge. She took a deep breath and willed herself to relax. She started back up the steps but didn't get far before a faint, muffled voice echoed up the stairwell.

Heart tripping, Paige strained her ear to listen.

A long second ticked by. Then she heard it again, a voice reverberating off the concrete walls and up through the stairwell. It sounded like her name.

Fear slashed through Paige. Once again, her mind flashed to the accident the night before. Would someone be so brazen as to come after her in broad daylight? In a busy shopping area?

At the thought, her pulse ratcheted higher. She didn't plan to wait around and see. She hurtled up the stairs to the next landing but halted as another thought sprang to life. What if it wasn't her name she'd heard but a cry for help?

Before she let fear seep back in, Paige spun around and grabbed hold of the railing. "Hello? Is everything okay?" she called out, pitching her voice to carry through the stairwell.

In the silence that followed her ear picked up a deep raspy breath. A longer pause and then *thump, thump, thump.* Pounding footsteps, emulating the deep thrum of her own heartbeat.

Fresh panic spiraled through her as Seth's words raced through her head: *Don't wait until something goes wrong. If you feel uncomfortable in a situation, get out of there.*

When would she learn? Yesterday, she'd wasted too much time analyzing the situation and she'd ended up in a ravine.

Lord, help me. Paige zigged and zagged up two more flights as footsteps pounded from behind her. Her shoulder bag banged into her side, spurring her on. Out of breath, she hit the fifth-floor landing and flung open the door.

Whack! The sound echoed as the metal door met resistance, followed by, "Hey! Watch it."

A surge of surprise jumbled with relief swept over Paige at the sound of the deep, rich baritone voice. But when the man stepped around the door, her knees weakened at the sight of him. Seth Garrison.

More and more Seth wished he'd just stayed out of town. Even better, he wished Paige had stayed in Durham. They hadn't seen each other in over ten months, and now he couldn't stay out of her way. Literally.

"Hello, Paige," Seth said, taking a step forward and holding his hand under his nose to keep the deluge of crimson from pouring out.

"Seth... I'm so sorry." Paige stared at him, color rising in her cheeks. "Oh, my. You're bleeding." She dug a handful of Art's Bistro napkins out of her purse, shoving them at him. "I hope you're okay."

He'd live. He sniffed and took the napkins, wiping his nose. Although he had to admit being on the receiving end of Paige's concern helped dull the pain some. He smiled briefly to ease her mind. "Nothing's broken. However, I hope throwing doors open like that isn't part of your new routine."

"No—no. Of course not." Paige swallowed and shot a nervous glance at him. "I was just in hurry."

"So I gathered." Seth stilled, gazing at her. Something flickered in her eyes; it wasn't just anxiety but fear, putting Seth's nerves on edge. A protective feeling welled up inside him, liquefying his resolve to keep his distance and stay out of her business.

He started to ask her a question, then stopped as a coldness seeped through him as common sense reasserted itself.

Protecting or even consoling Paige wasn't his responsibility. She'd just had him thrown off her case. She didn't want his help or concern.

And he didn't need the frustration. Let her new detective, Brett Ralston, take care of that.

Seth weighed that rationale for a split second before concern for Paige won out. No matter that the relationship between them had grown cold, he still cared about her. "So what's going on that's made you in such a hurry?"

Paige stared back at him, her brow knitted. "I'm probably just being paranoid, but I think someone may have been following me."

"Following you?" Concern crawled up Seth's spine. He wiped his hands and trashed the napkins in a bin by the wall. "Let me take a look."

Brushing past Paige, Seth stepped into the stairwell. Automatically, he moved his arm to feel the reassuring bulge of his Glock 23 beneath his leather jacket, nestled in its shoulder holster.

Not that he expected to need it, but he'd learned long ago during his navy SEAL training the value of taking precautions.

Sunlight streamed in from the open door behind him, illuminating the typically dim space. He crossed the narrow landing in three strides as a dull pounding echoed from below, the sound of heavy-booted feet on the metal stairs.

Seth leaned over the balustrade and peered down the stairwell to the ground floor. He glimpsed a shadow moving down the steps. His heartbeat kicked up. Maybe Paige wasn't being paranoid.

Patterns of short labored breaths echoed back to him through the center stairwell. A moment later, a dark figure loomed into view. He appeared to look around before he stepped from the stairwell onto the concrete first floor.

Seth craned his neck for a better look. *Male. Sturdy build. Baseball cap.* He watched as the man threw a fleeting glance back up the staircase before he turned and sprinted away, disappearing into the shadows.

Alarm slithered up Seth's spine. He spun and exploded into a run even before he heard the ground-floor door slam. Bypassing Paige, he headed down a row of parked cars toward the east side of the fifth-floor lot.

"What's going on?" Paige called to him.

Without stopping, he yelled back, "Check the front lot and see if anyone is getting into a vehicle or leaving. And let me know what kind of vehicle they're driving."

Seth skidded to an abrupt halt at the block wall at the back edge of the parking deck. Grabbing the edge firmly, he lurched forward and looked down into the lot below, anticipating a dead end. There was a plethora of outdoor parking; the guy could be anywhere. But Seth hoped this remote lot would be the top choice for someone wanting to be out of the public eye.

Seth's heart rate surged when his hunch paid off and he spotted a man in a ball cap scurry across the parking lot to a white Ford pickup and climb inside.

Could this be the same vehicle that ran Paige off the mountain?

Extended cab. Long bed. Seth grabbed his phone to get a picture. As he adjusted his camera to zero in, the truck took off out of the lot and barreled around the corner. A fresh burst of anger burned in Seth's gut.

Who is this guy? He gritted his teeth as that question slammed into his brain.

Turning his head, he saw Paige hurrying toward him.

"What is it?" she asked, her eyes wide.

Seth took an uneasy breath and pocketed his cell phone. "I saw someone in the stairwell. He left through the ground-floor exit. I had hoped to get a look at him."

"Did you see him?" Paige glanced over her shoulder to the parking lot below.

"Only a glimpse," Seth said. "Just before he took off in a white pickup."

Her startled green gaze swung back to him. "Long bed and extended cab?"

He nodded, still trying to catch his breath.

"I knew it." She breathed in, issuing a tremulous smile of relief. "It has to be the same creep that ran me off the road."

Despite the concern weighing heavy in his chest, Seth smiled back. Everything was speculative, but Paige's in- tuition about someone trying to hurt her was taking on more credibility. The question was, who was that someone? "I'll make sure to update Detective Ralston on what happened today, now that *he's* the detective on your case."

Paige brightened further, offering a short nod. She didn't seem to notice his little dig. Not that she owed him anything. Although, given the way their conversation went last night, it was probably just as well he wasn't running her investigation. They'd butted heads more than they'd discussed her case. Hardly productive.

"Now that we have a possible make and color of a vehicle, will that be enough to narrow down a suspect?"

Seth heard the hope in her voice, and as he looked up, she took a step closer. He caught the scent of her perfume. Vanilla.

Soothing and sweet. The Paige he remembered.

And with her sweet scent came a slew of uninvited memories, a blast of slide-show images flashing in his mind. But rather than letting them linger, Seth squashed them, slamming the book on that chapter of his life. Some things in life couldn't be undone. And a failed relationship was one of them.

Yep. Good thing he wasn't on her case.

Seth unclenched his teeth and eased back a step, putting some more distance between them. "We're dealing with a very common vehicle. Things could take time."

Paige deflated a little. "I guess it wasn't much of a lead after all."

"It's a start and will get the ball rolling." Seth came back, adding, "Every clue matters." At least to him. Although he was no longer running Paige's investigation.

Her lips quirked upward, and she brightened again.

The knot of uneasiness in Seth's gut ballooned into a boulder at Paige's easy smile. Even in his attempt to encourage her, he worried she wasn't concerned enough about her own safety. Instead, she focused on saving her brother—at all costs. Seth sighed, folding his arms over his chest. "In the meantime, Paige, you should consider going back to Durham to lie low for a while, at least until after Trey's trial."

"You're kidding," Paige said, a bewildered expression on her face as if she couldn't believe what she'd just heard. "Unless my brother's case will be reopened and the investigation into Madison's murder gets underway again, I won't be going anywhere."

Seth unfolded his arms, stuffing his hands in the pockets of his bomber jacket, wishing she'd be reasonable. "Under the present circumstances, I don't think it's a good idea to hang around and wait on that possibility."

Paige looked at him, her brows scrunched tight. "Someone in Boone obviously wants me dead. Shouldn't that alone cast some doubt on my brother's guilt? At least enough to get Madison's murder investigation rolling again?"

Seth shifted his weight with a deep breath, an ache settling in his chest as he thought of a more probable explanation for Paige's attacks. Vengeance.

Tempers flared back to life among Boone residents at the news of Trey's upcoming trial. Everyone in town was talking about it. And what better way to get back at Trey Becker than by hurting his sister?

"Paige, we'll need more evidence to cast doubt on what we've already collected. What I'm more concerned about right now is the possibility of someone trying to hurt you as a means to get back at your—" He didn't get a chance to fully explain before Paige's expression morphed from bewilderment to red-hot anger.

"I can't believe this," she snapped, shaking her head, a frown marring her beautiful face. "I doubt there's anything that would convince you that my brother's not guilty."

Not true. All that was needed was evidence. But Seth didn't bother with a response. They'd beat that dead horse enough already. "Paige, I'd like you to consider leaving town. I don't think Trey would want you to sacrifice your safety in his defense."

Paige didn't flinch at the comment, nor did she respond. Instead she merely looked at her watch and then back at him. "I need to get going. It's getting late, and I've taken up enough of your time. I appreciate you looking out for me today."

Before he could respond, she was halfway down the row of vehicles, heading to hers.

Frustration roared up in him. Wrangling it back, he watched as she climbed into her rental sedan. He had to stop himself from going after her. He knew nothing he could say would change her mind about anything.

Seth headed down the parking garage stairs to Art's Bistro, where his takeout order was ready and waiting for him. Although, his appetite was no longer raging—concern for Paige had taken care of that.

God if You're still out there, watch over Paige. The prayer came out nowhere, surprising even him. He hadn't talked to God in years, but Seth hoped He was listening.

Paige was going to need it.

THREE

Something startled Paige out of a sound sleep.

For a moment she lay stock-still, heart racing, listening. Distant thunder rumbled, and relief settled in.

Stop being paranoid. Paige sighed and rolled to her side. As she snuggled more comfortably beneath the down comforter, she glanced at the bedside clock. Eight fifteen.

She pushed aside her blankets and forced her still-achy body out of bed. Flipping on the light, a yellow glow flooded the room. So much for getting an early start.

She went straight to her suitcase, and as she started to unzip it, she caught her reflection in the dresser mirror, realizing she'd fallen asleep in her clothes.

Lord, help me get it together.

A creak and then something thumped, and she froze again.

Was someone in the house?

The floor creaked again, raising the hair on the back of her neck. She launched toward the bedroom door, pushing it shut and twisting the lock.

Her mind raced, keeping time with her thundering heart. She needed to do something. Call someone. *Nine-one-one.* No, Brett Ralston.

She spun back to the bedside and snatched her new phone from the side table, punching the one number on her list of contacts.

Teeth clenched, she pressed the handset against her ear, clasping tighter on each unanswered ring. *Lord, let him answer.*

A series of dull thumps. *Footsteps!*

A surge of panic fired through her. The ringing stopped, and Brett's voice mail picked up. "Sorry I missed you—"

She slammed the disconnect key and then fumbled with her phone, trying to dial 911.

A faint thud sounded, then another, followed by an electrifying rumble as lightning flashed against the closed window blinds.

Fear exploded through Paige as a frantic scream tangled in her lungs. She swallowed against her suddenly dry throat as her knees buckled. She planted her hand on the bedside table to keep from toppling over, prayers flying heavenward. *Lord, help me.*

"Paige?"

Blinking, Paige's breath caught. She shoved the phone back on her ear. "Brett?"

"Paige. Are you okay?"

Paige swung around on her toes, and her eyes riveted to the closed door, the cell phone dangling from her fingers. "Brett? Is that you?"

"Yes. It's me."

She rushed to the door then halted. What was Brett doing there? Before she could fully ponder the question, he answered it for her.

"I stopped by to see how you were doing."

Her confidence in Brett continued to soar. "Thank

you—" She stopped, jarred by another thought. "Brett, how did you get inside the condo?"

"I knocked, and when you didn't answer I tried the door and it was unlocked." His deep voice carried through the wood door.

Brett's words rattled around her head. *Unlocked?* She'd made two trips to her car for groceries, but could she have been so distracted she'd forgotten to lock the door?

Her chest tightened. This ordeal with her brother was making her crazy.

"Paige. Are you okay?"

Without answering, she twisted the lock and pulled open the door. Breath froze in her lungs as Brett appeared in her line of sight, his deep-set eyes narrowing as he stared down at her, a black revolver clasped in his hand.

"You really need to be more careful about locking your doors." Brett holstered his gun, and she breathed again.

"You're right." She nodded, hand to her heart as if she could slow the frantic beat. "I've just been so distracted." And exhausted and frazzled.

"Understood." Brett's expression was guarded as always, but his fair eyes remained somewhat skeptical. "I received a message from Seth last night. He told me about yesterday's parking-deck incident. He's pretty concerned about you. Sounds like you had another scare."

A lump settled in Paige's throat as she thought about Seth. She'd let frustration get the best of her yesterday, and once again her conversation with him ended on a sour note. And despite it all he was still concerned about her.

Lord, help me to be more gracious when it comes to Seth.

"And, from what Seth told me, I'm inclined to agree with him," Brett continued, folding his arms over his chest. "The best idea would be for you to head back home and hang low for a while."

Raw emotions bubbled up inside her, flowing through her veins like molten lava. Her brother's life was at stake. Didn't anyone get that? "Brett, I can't do that."

Brett had been supportive after her brother's arrest. He'd been a close friend of Trey's. Even after she'd left town, he made an effort to call and check in with her. If anyone should understand her motives to stay, he should.

Paige straightened, tossing her bedraggled curls over her shoulders. "Brett, everyone seems to agree that my life is in danger. Isn't that enough to raise suspicion that maybe Madison's killer is still out there? And open up a new avenue in her murder investi—"

"That's not my call," Brett snapped before she could finish. "We can't assume anything until there's concrete evidence to back it up. But be assured the Watauga County Sheriff's Department has a strong team of detectives. They'll dig into this. And the best thing for you to do in the meantime is go home to Durham."

Of course he'd think that. Paige blew out an impatient breath. She'd hoped, but never directly asked, if Brett thought her brother was innocent. The one advocate she *thought* she had.

"I appreciate your concern, Brett," she said, forcing a warm smile. "But I've learned my lesson. I plan to keep my cell phone close and my doors locked. I'll keep an eye on my surroundings, and at the first sign of trouble I'll call for help."

Brett's thick blond brows knit above his prominent nose. "I wish you'd let this go, Paige, and let the courts handle it."

Perfect cop lingo. Easy advice for someone with nothing to lose. "Thank you, Brett. And you'll keep me posted on any progress on my case?"

Brett tilted his head and tightened his arms. "There's no convincing you, is there?"

She hesitated a long moment and then shook her head. "No, sorry." She managed another small grin. "But, about the investigation…"

Brett unfolded his arms and rested his hands on his waist. "I already have people searching county records for the make and model of the pickup that was seen yesterday. We'll be looking closely at the owners and their possible connection to the Cramer family. If I find out anything, I'll let you know."

She felt better already. With a steadying breath, she went with Brett to the door, locking it after he walked out. She slumped down at the table in the kitchen, the dash of hope, the determination she'd brought along with her to Boone, starting to wane.

She'd expected Seth to balk at the idea that her would-be killer was also the same person who killed Madison, but even Brett brushed off her theory.

Which only brought the truth into razor-sharp focus.

Cops thrived on hard facts. Gut feelings weren't enough.

Right now, all she had was her gut.

Seth jerked awake, his heart racing and his body covered in sweat. *Again.* This had been going on all night long. Falling asleep only to be woken within the hour, his acid-drenched stomach clenched in knots as his foggy brain struggled against nightmarish images—flashbacks of a horrific crime scene the night Madison was murdered.

The scene was like Seth remembered. A dimly lit room. The hum of anguished sobs nearly drowned out by the wail of police sirens outside the house. Trey Becker cowering beside a lifeless body, a ring of blood pooled around her. In his nightmare, every detail was eerily consistent to Madison's murder—except the victim was Paige Becker.

A sick feeling chilled Seth to the bone, even as he continued to remind himself it was only a dream.

Fighting a groan, he rolled to his side and glanced at the red numbers on the bedside clock, sighing when he read nine o'clock. He'd slept in and still felt exhausted.

Flopping onto his back, he scrubbed his face with his hands as if he was able to scrub the horrible image out of his brain. During his career as a navy SEAL, he'd witnessed countless vicious events and battled his share of nightmares because of it.

But the feeling of foreboding that accompanied this dream he couldn't shake. If anything ever happened to Paige, he'd—

Stop it! Seth sat up in bed. He wasn't responsible for keeping Paige safe, he coached himself firmly. She didn't need his help. Didn't want his help.

He always felt better after a dose of levelheaded rationale.

But not today.

Seth blew out a frustrated breath, jaw clenching as he snagged his cell off the bedside table. Worrying about Paige was unproductive.

As he scrolled through his emails, he mentally prioritized the messages in order of importance and tried to stay focused. But thoughts of Paige kept tumbling back, and along with those thoughts came several nagging questions.

If someone was trying to hurt her, who was it? One of Madison's family members? An angry neighbor? A friend? Even more important, what was Brett's plan to protect Paige?

Last night Seth had left a message for Brett about Paige's parking deck scare. Brett texted him a quick thank-you, but Seth had hoped for a call back. It wasn't that he didn't have faith in Brett's ability as a detective, but he'd feel better knowing the details for Brett's strategy on solving Paige's case.

Seth eyed the list of messages again. Maybe Brett had called and he'd missed it. He scrolled one more time down the page to the end. Nada.

A heavy sigh escaped him as he tossed the phone on the bed. Brett didn't have any obligation to keep him in the loop. Not that Seth blamed him. Paige didn't want him around. Brett probably knew that.

For the next minute, Seth just sat there, jaw clenched, the ceiling fan whirring lazily overhead as he ordered himself to get a grip. He needed to forget about the case. Period.

This was going to be a long couple weeks. Groaning under his breath, he got up and pulled on some jeans. If nothing else, he could satisfy his growling stomach.

He stopped midstride on his way to the kitchen as a thought came to him. Nothing said he couldn't call and check in on a friend. If nothing else, that's what Paige was. A friend. He hoped she thought the same of him.

Without further speculation, Seth pivoted back and grabbed his phone. He punched in Paige's number, surprised at how quickly it came back to him. Which meant nothing, he told himself, other than his navy-ingrained memory skills were still sharply intact.

Three…four…five…

Seth counted the rings, about to hang up, when Paige finally picked up.

"Hello."

Relief flowed, and Seth sank down on the edge of the bed. "Good morning, Paige."

For a long moment, taut silence stretched across the line. Finally she said, "Seth? Is that you?"

He heard a degree of trepidation in her voice. "Yes. I didn't wake you, did I?"

"No—no, I was awake."

Seth paused, giving her a moment to say more. Instead more awkward silence hung on the line. "Good. I'm glad I didn't wake you." He scowled at the conversation, or lack of. "I just wanted to call and make sure everything was okay."

Paige's heated sigh sizzled through the phone line. "I don't think anything in my life will be *okay* until Madison's killer is caught and my brother is free."

Seth mentally kicked himself. He'd set himself up for that one. He shifted the cell to his other ear, tried again. "How are you feeling from the accident?" A more pointed question.

Another sigh, but less heated. "Other than being a little stiff, I feel better, thank you."

"Good." Now, if she would only hightail it back to Durham, he'd feel better. "Paige, I'd like to talk to you about your decision to stay in Boone. I really don't think it's a good idea, especially after—" He was trying to tread lightly around the sensitive subject, but she shut him down quickly.

"Seth, I need to get going. I have a full agenda today."

Of course she does. Seth swallowed a snort. *Trouble.* That's what he saw on her agenda. She was setting herself up for more grief and pain...or worse. "Paige, you really need to go back to Durham." So much for treading lightly.

"I'm not leaving, Seth."

Seth's jaw tightened as he willed away the protective anger that was building in his chest. "Paige, two days ago someone ran you off the road and yesterday someone was following you. Aren't you concerned about your safety?"

"I'm concerned about my brother."

"Well, I'm concerned about you."

Silence.

Seth ran an agitated hand through his hair, remembering a time when talking to Paige was anything but awkward. A time when she was rational. But that time wasn't now.

"Paige—"

"I have to go."

Before he could say more, she disconnected.

An hour later, Seth hunkered down behind the computer in his office, nursing a strong cup of coffee as he read over Trey Becker's case file.

The click of the doorknob, and his office door opened, breaking his concentration. Seth peered over the top of the computer screen as Detective Ted Hanson stood in the doorway.

"I thought I saw a light on in here."

Seth smirked and lifted a brow. "And you didn't think to knock?"

A chuckle rumbled from deep in Ted's chest. "I suppose I would have, had I thought you'd actually be here. What happened to not stepping a foot back in this place until you used up every minute of your vacation days?"

He'd obviously been talking to the chief. Seth glared at his friend. "Don't ask."

"Can't stop thinking about Paige's case, huh?"

Ted was a lifelong buddy; they'd both grown up in Raleigh before leaving to attend Appalachian State University in Boone. And after Seth's stint in the navy, Ted recruited him to the sheriff's department. Ted was a good man, thick as a bear, all muscle, and didn't believe in beating around the bush.

Still, Seth ignored his comment. The truth was, Ted was right. He couldn't stop thinking about Paige, period. A fact he hated to even admit to himself. "You know Ralston's on the case."

"Yeah, I heard." Ted leaned against the doorjamb. "Although I also heard he's working on a strong lead."

Seth set down his cup and rocked back in his chair. "He's on the hunt for a white Ford extended-cab pickup."

"Wow." Ted whistled softly between his teeth. "There's no shortage of those around here."

"No kidding."

"Any suspects?"

"Nope."

Ted folded his arms across his chest. "Do you really think someone's targeting Paige?"

Seth shifted in his swivel chair, elbows propped on the arms. After a moment, he nodded and gave his one-word conclusion. "Yes."

"And all you have going for you is a make and color of a truck." Ted shook his head. "Buddy, you have your work cut out for you."

A pang of uneasy worry tightened Seth's gut, but he shoved it away. He rocked back farther in his chair and intertwined his fingers behind his head. "Tell that to Ralston. It's not my case."

Ted gave a short, amused laugh. "Maybe not officially. But you're not here on your day off for nothing. Let me guess what you're looking over."

Ted was also perceptive. Just not always right. "It's not Paige's case," Seth said with a wry smile.

"Really?" Ted's brown eyes narrowed. "So, then what are you doing here?"

Seth had asked himself the same question more than once since he arrived. "I'm looking over Trey Becker's files."

"Trey Becker?" Ted echoed, then added, "I thought the case against him was airtight."

"Just looking over it with fresh eyes. Brainstorming." Seth rocked forward and shrugged. "Probably a waste of time." But he wanted to make sure the case was as rock solid as he remembered, secured by evidence and not assumptions.

Ted nodded. "The good news is, Trey's trial is in less than two weeks. So Paige shouldn't be in town long. In the meantime, where's she staying?"

Thirteen long days. Seth bit back a smirk. He looked at Ted. "She's staying at a friend's condo at Beaver Creek."

"That's good. A gated community." Ted nodded again. "I heard that patrol cars were making extra rounds in the area last night. Ralston must have ordered that."

Seth wished Ralston had been so proactive. He shook his head. "Ralston didn't. I did." Seth thought he'd sleep better with beefed-up security in the condo area. He was wrong.

Ted's laugh rumbled through the room as he walked out the door. "And you're not on Paige's case? Right. You might want to buddy up with Ralston on this one."

"No. Ralston's got it." For now. Seth planned to keep his eye on things from a distance. Like it or not, Paige didn't want him around.

The bell tinkled over the aged wooden door when Paige stepped into Cramer's Antique and Gift Mart, a quaint shop filled with not only antique treasures, but also floral arrangements, gourmet treats and unique works of art.

Several steps inside, Paige's nose picked up the rich scents of dark chocolate and fresh flowers mingling with old polished wood. An aroma that on any other day might have been appealing. But today a wave of nausea overtook her.

Paige swallowed against it, hoping she wasn't wasting her time coming here. Originally, she had planned to get in touch with Madison's friends and coworkers and distance herself from the Cramer family. But without the list of contact information she had on her phone, she was left with no choice but to stop by the family business to make those connections.

Paige said a quick prayer that she wasn't overstepping her boundaries and that she'd learn something new. Anything. A single clue. One little piece to the puzzle. She'd be happy with that.

Every clue matters. Seth's words played in her head. A warm feeling washed through her, and she felt a momentary twinge of peace. Inwardly she smiled. One clue at a time, and God would lead her to the truth.

Paige heard muffled steps. She looked to the right as a tall thirtysomething woman in jeans and a purple sweatshirt rounded the corner, a potted plant in her hand. The woman stiffened and froze when she saw Paige. Her eyebrows gathering over her wide, challenging stare confirmed Paige's greatest fear.

She wasn't welcome. Her heart throbbed. So far, she'd met opposition at every juncture. Trembling yet determined, Paige swallowed around the lump in her throat and forced her feet forward. Feigning nonchalance, she extended her hand. "Good morning. I'm Paige—"

"I know who you are, Miss Becker." The woman,

whose badge read Amy, slid the pot onto the counter beside the register. "I saw your picture in yesterday's paper."

Great. She'd probably made front-page news—*Trey Becker's Sister Runs Off Mountain Pass*. She bit back a sigh.

"And I don't think it's a good idea for you to be here," Amy continued in a low, strained voice as she craned her head to glance over her shoulder.

In that split second Paige felt the anxiety in the room ratchet higher. She followed Amy's glance to an open doorway at the rear of the shop.

Icy tingles skipped up Paige's spine. "Is Mrs. Cramer in?"

"No." A grimace took hold of Amy's face. "Mrs. Cramer hasn't worked since Madison's death. She can't even step into the shop. Everything around here reminds her of her daughter."

Paige's heart surged, touched by Mrs. Cramer's grief. This wasn't fair. A mother losing her daughter. No mother deserved that. She fought back the memories of Madison's brutal murder, sudden tears biting her eyes. *Lord, somehow bring Mrs. Cramer comfort.* "I'm very sorry to hear about Mrs. Cramer. I know her heart is broken."

"It has been hard for everyone," Amy replied tightly as sadness crept into her hazel eyes. "And I'm sorry about your brother."

The unexpected words wrapped around Paige like a hug. "Thank you," she said, taking a long breath. Then she remembered something Trey had told her. A close friend of Madison's, Amy Miles, had informed police that someone had been stalking Madison before she died. An allegation Trey was now suspected of. Was this the same Amy?

It was hard for Paige to keep the quaver out of her

voice as she asked Amy about her relationship with Madison.

Grabbing a pair of pruning shears, Amy worked as she spoke in a hushed tone, pausing one time to glance back at the doorway. "We were close," she started. "At times, like sisters. But there were things about Madison I just couldn't figure out."

Interest piqued, Paige took a step closer. "What kind of things?"

"Well—" Amy shrugged as she continued to snip brown tips off the leafy houseplant. "Madison's impulsiveness, for one. She would jump feetfirst into something only to later try and backpedal out of the situation."

"Like her relationship with my brother?" Paige muttered, mostly to herself. Madison and Trey's whirlwind romance had gone from dating to married in a matter of weeks. They'd eloped without even planning a wedding. Less than a year later they were separated, her brother's heart broken.

Amy stopped pruning, and she met Paige's gaze. "Yes, Madison jumped into the marriage. But Trey wasn't the problem. Being committed to anything or anyone scared Madison to death." She set down the shears. "But Madison did love Trey. I'd hoped things would work out for them."

The words slashed through Paige. After Trey and Madison separated, Paige rallied around Trey, struck by the hurt he was dealing with, never considering his wife's pain. Madison had suffered the loss of her father when she was a teen. A traumatic loss that could affect a victim's ability to form healthy relationships throughout a lifetime.

A deep sadness swept through Paige, trailed by guilt. She'd counseled women with similar issues. Why hadn't she thought to reach out to Madison?

Before regret got the best of her, Paige took a calming breath. The past couldn't be erased. She needed to concentrate on the future. Trey's future. She cleared her throat. "Amy, do you believe my brother killed Madison?"

Amy's eyes went wide, and her pale complexion turned impossibly paler. "I don't know what to believe."

Hope wrapped around Paige's heart and squeezed. *I don't know* meant there was some doubt in Amy's mind. Unlike other narrow-minded, judgmental townsfolk who already had her brother tried and sentenced. Seth included.

Hiking her purse strap higher on her shoulder, Paige pressed on. "Did Madison ever tell you she thought someone was stalking her?"

Amy grimaced and shook her head. "Miss Becker, you really should go. Madison's brother will be in soon and wouldn't be happy to see you here."

She could understand Gentry having hard feelings. He believed Trey had killed his sister, but hopefully he'd understand that she was just looking for the truth. "Amy, if you'll just answer a few more questions, I'd be so appreciative."

"I've already said more than I should have."

Actually, she hadn't said enough. Paige hesitated a moment and then shrugged. "I'm just trying to make sense of it all. Trey is my brother and—"

"I get it," Amy cut her off with a harsh whisper. "To answer your question, yes, Madison mentioned a couple weeks before she was killed that at times she felt like she was being followed."

"Why didn't she go to the police?" *Whoa.* Paige took a deep, bracing breath. She was starting to sound like Seth.

Amy locked eyes with Paige. A kind of impatient stare that said, *listen closely. I'm only going to say this once.*

"Madison second-guessed everything in her life and in this case, she kept going back to the notion that she was just being paranoid." Amy started clipping again. "I guess I didn't take it serious enough, either. Otherwise, I would have pressed her to contact law enforcement."

"Amy, it's not your fault." Paige was also good at second-guessing. A dangerous practice, as she was finding out. She sighed and crossed her arms. "Did Madison ever convey to you that she thought Trey might be stalking her?"

A quick wag of Amy's head sent adrenaline skipping through Paige. "No, she never implied anything like that to me, and I told the detectives the same thing." Picking up the shears, she pointed them at Paige. "Miss Becker, please understand, Trey was the one person Madison did trust."

A mixture of sorrow and confusion flooded through Paige. Madison loved and trusted Trey but she'd walked away from their relationship. No wonder Trey was depressed.

But, if Madison didn't think of Trey as a threat, had there been someone else she was afraid of?

Paige took a step even closer. "Amy, was there anyone you can think of that Madison had an issue with? Or maybe had an issue with her?"

"Really, Miss Becker, you should leave now." Amy stopped clipping. She didn't make eye contact. "I've told the detectives everything I—"

"Paige, what are you doing here?" The gruff male voice boomed from the back of the store, silencing Amy and sending Paige's heart into spasms.

Paige jerked her gaze back to the doorway, freezing on Gentry Cramer's face. His dark stare drilled her as he shoved his phone in his pocket and came nearer, not breaking his stride as he stalked around old pieces of furniture and display cases, chest puffed out, muscles flexed. A taller, stocky man she didn't recognize followed him.

"Gentry, how are you?" Paige asked in a strained voice. The sick feeling in her gut just intensified. She hadn't expected a warm reception—Gentry had never been overly friendly to her, even before his sister's death—but his anger was even deeper than she'd suspected. But as he was fighting for justice for his sibling, she was also fighting for hers. Maybe he could understand that?

"Good morning, Gentry. Good morning, Eli." Amy spoke up, a slight quiver in her voice. "Miss Becker just stopped in to see Mrs. Cramer. I told her your mother wasn't here and she was just getting ready to leave."

"My mother?" Gentry growled, his mouth hardening to a straight line. "She can barely get out of bed these days. The last thing she needs is to be confronted by the sister of her daughter's killer."

Paige's heart nearly burst wide-open, just hearing the word *killer*. The one word she hated to be used in conjunction with her brother. *What happened to innocent until proven guilty?* That question burned deep in her mind, but instead of shouting it out, she breathed deep, willing herself to calm down. Now wasn't the time to make that point. "Actually Gentry, I stopped by with hopes of speaking to some of Madison's coworkers. I know how hard her death has been on your family, and I'm so sorry for your loss. It would never be my intention to upset your mother or anyone else, however—"

"Then get out." Gentry's voice snapped like a too-taut elastic band as he gestured sharply with one long-fingered hand toward the door.

His counterpart, Eli, took a step, plunking curled fists

on his hips. "Miss Becker, you need to leave. Let me walk you out."

"That's not necessary," Paige said, clutching her purse closer to her side. She spun on her heel and headed for the door. Heart thumping, she was shaking inside. Perplexed. This was crazy. She swallowed around tears clogging her throat. Both she and Gentry wanted the same thing—for Madison's killer to be brought to justice. She couldn't just walk away.

Frustration peaking and acting purely on adrenaline, she stopped short, wheeled around and turned her gaze back on Gentry.

The intensity in his expression as he glared back at her made it difficult for her to even breathe; still, she went on. "Gentry, if justice is what you're seeking, please listen to what I have to say." Paige tried to keep her voice from shaking. "I know there's a mountain of alleged evidence stacked against Trey, but he never would have hurt Madison. I really believe her murderer is still out there. If you'll just give me three minutes, I'll explain."

The scowl on Gentry's face never wavered. Just that same contorted expression and narrow-eyed stare, like she was out of her mind. "You've overstayed your welcome, Paige."

The sound of sirens pierced the air. Her heart stopped, then burst into a savage beat when she glanced behind her and out the window at the flashing red, blue and white lights of the deputy cruiser parked right outside.

Just when she thought things couldn't get worse.

"What do you mean, Paige has been arrested?" Seth shot out of his chair, dropping his half-eaten sandwich on his desk.

"Deputy Hobbs brought her in about an hour ago," Ted said, dogging Seth's steps as he stalked out of his office and down the hallway that would take him outside the building.

"And what's she been charged with?"

"Misdemeanor trespassing."

Seth stopped short, one hand on the exit doors, and looked at Ted. "Trespassing? Where was she?"

"Cramer's Antiques."

He should have known.

Seth pushed through the exit and headed across the street to the jail.

Clouds had gathered overhead, and a light icy drizzle was falling. Seth took an inhale of cold, moist air, which did nothing to diffuse the heat building inside him as he wondered what kind of trouble Paige would get herself into next.

Inside the county jail, he took the elevator down one level to the basement, then entered a long, dark corridor that led to the magistrate's office. Pushing through a second set of double wooden doors, he entered the courtroom. He allowed his gaze to cruise the front three rows of seats, about half-filled with suspects waiting for their preliminary hearing before the magistrate. Paige was right there among them.

As Seth took a seat in the back row, Paige was called to a podium to have her charges read—criminal trespassing in the second degree.

Deputy Ed Hobbs stood to the side and explained to the judge how Paige had unlawfully remained on the Cramer's Antique and Gift Mart's property after the owner, Gentry Cramer, made several reasonable requests for her to leave.

A bogus charge, in Seth's opinion.

Three minutes later the judge banged his gavel, set a court date for next month and released Paige on her own recognizance with no bail.

Seth hung in the back of the room and waited.

After signing for her personal items to be returned, Paige bolted down the aisle and out of the courtroom, her purse clutched at her side.

"Hey, Detective." Deputy Ed Hobbs caught up with Seth just outside the courtroom doors as he headed out after her. "Sorry about all this."

Seth stopped, leveling his gaze on Hobbs. "Sorry about all what?"

Hobbs's eyebrows went up a notch. "Taking Miss Becker into custody. I know you guys used to be—"

"Never mind about that, Hobbs." Seth waved a hand. "I just wish you could have handled things without an arrest."

Hobbs shifted uneasily, eyes wide. "She was on the property when I arrived. And Mr. Cramer said—"

"Forget it," Seth said. "What's done is done." He clapped a hand on his shoulder. "You did what you thought you had to do." And maybe it would deter Paige some.

Then again, probably not.

Seth took the stairs to the first floor and caught up with Paige as she exited through the glass doors leading outside. "Hey, do you need a lift?"

Paige stopped and turned around. He thought he detected a relieved expression even as she frowned at him. "Yes, if you don't mind. I suppose I need one."

"Okay, then let's get out of here." He jerked his thumb toward the staff parking lot.

As they walked across the street, Seth listened to Paige's side of the story.

Unfortunately, her experience was nothing less than he expected, minus the 911 call.

"I feel terrible about what happened to Madison, and I understand Gentry's grief. But whoever heard of being arrested for trying to talk to someone?" Paige pulled her wool coat tighter around her and tugged on the sash.

"I think there was a lot more emotion involved than reason to arrest you." Seth tucked his hands in his coat pockets.

"Good. Tell that to the judge, because he just set my court date for next month."

Seth glanced at Paige, staring straight ahead, the frigid breeze rustling stray locks of hair around her face. So beautiful. So dedicated and loyal. An overwhelming need to protect her welled up inside him. Seth fought it back. Concern was one thing, but he needed to keep his feelings and emotions in check. "I'll talk to your attorney."

"I don't have an attorney." Paige's frown intensified, and Seth brushed his arm against hers to curb her concern.

"The court will appoint you one. And don't worry, I'll take care of it."

She risked a furtive glance and nodded. "Thank you." The sadness in her voice ripped Seth's heart to shreds. He didn't know who frustrated him more—Gentry for pressing charges against her, or Trey, who, willingly or not, dragged her into this whole mess.

Either way, both scenarios stank.

"I don't even know where to go from here," Paige said, her voice flat and emotionless. "I can't decide if Gentry is hiding something or just hates me because he believes Trey killed his sister."

Seth guessed the latter. There had never been a reason to suspect Madison's brother of any connection to his sister's death. But, then again, someone was after Paige, and right now everyone was a suspect. "Have you talked to Brett about what happened today?"

Tucking her fisted hands in her coat pockets, she shrugged. "Yes. I was able to make one phone call, so I called him. But there's nothing he could do. He said the trespassing charge wasn't related to my case. However, he may be looking at Gentry as a person of interest in my case."

"Good." Seth nodded, ignoring the little tug in his chest. It only made sense that she'd called Brett, but for some reason it still bugged him. Although he was happy with Brett's response. "So, what makes you think Gentry might be hiding something?"

"Amy Miles, the woman who works for him," Paige said, the concern in her voice escalating on each spoken word. "She was very uneasy when I arrived at the antique mart today. She said Gentry would be upset to see me there. He obviously doesn't keep his hatred for Trey or even me a secret from his staff."

Amy Miles. Seth knew that name. Stopping beside his truck, he thought back over the files he'd briefed today. He pulled open the passenger door for Paige. "Wasn't Miss Miles a close friend of Madison's?"

"Yes." Paige nodded and then proceeded to tell him about her conversation with Amy and how the woman appeared nervous, even apprehensive about talking to her. Once again Paige had a gut feeling that Amy suspected something, going on to say that Amy had doubts that Trey was Madison's killer.

Seth couldn't suppress his grimace. Wishing she'd stop trying to play detective and start worrying about her own safety.

A low rumble of thunder punctuated his thought.

Seth shut Paige's door as a light drizzle started to fall and then scrambled around the other side as his gut feeling said, *yeah right*.

Dread climbed up his back, ramping up his concern, and the urge to protect Paige roared up again. But no matter if he wanted to keep her safe, she wasn't about to let him back in her life, even on a temporary basis. That alone should have deterred him, but just knowing Paige's life was in jeopardy trumped any rationale he could come up with.

He was a doomed man.

FOUR

The ride to Paige's car dragged on forever. Paige shifted against the passenger seat, trying to keep her attention focused out the windshield. A thick silence hovered in the truck cab as neither she nor Seth attempted to make small talk. When she finally couldn't stand it any longer, she risked a glance at him, wondering what even possessed him to come by the magistrate's office. She knew his perspective about her being in Boone. And he wasn't an advocate.

What she saw as a loving sister's attempt to clear her brother's name, Seth characterized as a delusionary crusade, one that would only stir up anger among townsfolk and compromise her safety all at the same time.

And she had to admit certain points to his argument made sense, save one. Her mission wasn't delusionary. Because with every fiber of her being she believed Trey was innocent. Now all she had to do was find the evidence to prove it.

She drew in a deep breath to bolster her courage. She had a big job ahead of her.

If she hadn't known her brother's kind nature, strong family values and flawless integrity, she might have questioned his innocence herself. But she had no doubt in her mind that even in his darkest moments he would never be capable of what he was accused of.

The allegations just didn't make sense. Trey was an elite navy veteran who'd conducted covert operations throughout the most dangerous corners of the globe. Even if he *was* inclined to commit murder, he'd never be so careless as to leave behind a string of evidence. Regardless of the bout of depression he was battling or his recent loss of sobriety.

And the sad kicker Paige was still processing was that Trey hadn't had a drink in eight years, not since he'd found his way to sobriety in college after falling victim to alcohol addiction. Since then Trey had been fiercely against the use of any substance and had even served in the local schools as an antiaddiction advocate. He understood the effects of drugs and alcohol and that abusing them destroyed lives, including their parents'.

Paige swallowed hard around the sudden lump in her throat as she thought about what a black hole of despair her brother's life must have become for him to let his guard slip and pick up that first drink.

And that relapse cost him plenty. His sobriety, his reputation and possibly his freedom.

Sorrow for her brother quickly morphed into fear. Paige blinked away the sudden tears blurring her vision as she thought about the perils of Trey's future.

She hated to even fathom him spending the rest of his life behind bars. But reality was, unless there was new evidence in his defense, the probability of that happening was quite real. Today as she sat confined to the holding cell at the jail, she got a small taste of what her brother's living conditions had been for the last ten months. A closet-like concrete space, cold and lonely—a horrible existence, especially for someone innocent.

Paige pressed a hand to her lips to hold in a sigh. *Don't give in to fear*, she counseled herself firmly. She needed to stay strong for Trey's sake, but the giant fist squeezing her heart only served to remind her what she was up against.

Somewhere out there a murderer was on the loose, and she needed to find him.

"You okay?"

The deep, resonant sound of Seth's voice sent her thoughts splintering into a hundred directions. She jerked around to find him staring at her. Lines of concern creased his forehead as he gripped the steering wheel, waiting for the light to turn green.

"You seem pretty keyed up." He gestured to her hands. She looked down. Both were clenched into fists, squeezing so tight her knuckles blanched.

"Yeah, I guess I am." Paige quickly unclenched, flexed her fingers. "It's been a rough day, but I'm okay and trying to stay positive. Just a little glitch on the road to success." Even as she tried to sound lighthearted, Seth scowled.

"So you are planning to stay in town?"

Not this again. She looked away. "Of course. I don't have a choice but to stay and finish what I came to do." Now more than ever.

"Like I mentioned to you before, being in town, trying to dig up information to help Trey, isn't going to be easy for you. And, yes, Paige, you do have a choice."

So was that why he'd come by the magistrate's office? To remind her that she wasn't welcome back in Boone? Well, she'd already figured that out and wasn't leaving. Fighting a scowl herself, Paige didn't bother to respond, but instead she gazed at an invisible point in the distance, relieved when the light turned green and the truck started moving again. She didn't have the stamina to defend her motives at the moment. Seth didn't get it. He never would.

As they turned onto Queen Street, one by one the rustic antique gas streetlamps flickered to life, spilling a soft yellow glow across the parking area beside Cramer's Antique and Gift Mart.

Seth pulled into a parking spot several down from her rented sedan, shifted into Park and killed the engine. *Finally.* Paige barely resisted a sigh of relief as she started to unbuckle her seat belt.

Seth pushed open his door and then paused as the interior dome lights penetrated the dusk. "Paige, I know you think trying to help Trey is the right and noble thing to—"

"Please, Seth, don't—" She waved a hand. "I don't want to go through this again. I just need to get home." A long sigh slipped out. Then, pulling her purse on her lap, she riffled through it for her keys.

"Paige, listen to me, please," he demanded softly, and his voice, thick with emotion and concern, momentarily took her breath away.

With her pulse sprinting, Paige pulled in a deep breath, blew it out. How dare he catch her off guard like that. She'd much rather go up against that stubborn *just listen to me* spirit of his. Because at the moment, her stubborn *I'm not going to listen to you* spirit was seriously waning.

"Paige?"

Paige pulled out her keys, fisting them in her left hand. Reluctantly she lifted her gaze to meet his. "Seth, I know you don't approve of what I'm trying to do. But please try and understand that I can't leave Boone without answers."

He frowned, an anything but understanding look on his face. "I get that you want to help your brother. I just don't think you're going about it in the right way. Talk to his attorneys—"

"I have. They've given up." And her brother was also on the brink of giving up himself.

"Come on, Paige." Seth growled. He scrubbed a hand through his hair, frustration creasing the corners of his eyes. "This isn't your battle."

Really? Her stomach quivered at his statement. Then whose battle was it? Her brother was locked behind bars, and no one was fighting for him. "I tried to have faith in law enforcement and the justice system. But no one is giving us the answers we need."

"Maybe the answers you want aren't out there."

Paige's heart gave a solid kick. No, she'd never believe that. And the doubt she heard in Seth's tone only served to remind her why she needed to keep her distance from him. She needed to stay positive. Have faith. *Lord, help me stay on the right path. And open Seth's eyes to the truth.* About God and her brother.

"Thank you for the ride, Seth." She refrained from commenting further. She pushed open the truck door and jumped out. She took a deep breath, filled her lungs with fresh air, blew it out. Without even a glance back, she hurried to her rented sedan.

She needed to get on with her plans. With her life. Being around Seth made accomplishing both nearly impossible. He was like an overprotective father. But that was Seth. *Safety first.* An admirable quality, one she appreciated and actually practiced herself. But in this situation, he was way off base.

Plain and simple, her brother needed her help.

And although she wasn't naive enough to not take the threats against her seriously, she tried not to focus on them. She couldn't let fear take over.

Firmly reiterating that, Paige fumbled with her keys with shaking fingers.

From the corner of her eye, she saw Seth watching her. Whatever was left of her nerves shredded further. Why couldn't he be nice and just go? But instead he moved up beside her, gently steadying her hand. Instantly, warmth skittered through her extremities, and her heart jumped into a gallop. "Here, let me help."

Biting into her lip, she tried to hold it together as his thumb pressed the key fob and the door lock clicked.

"Thank you." She jerked her hand away as if he'd bitten her, still shaking from her reactions both to Seth's touch and the reality of having him around again. She took a step back, teeth gritted. She'd spent ten months reining in her own battered emotions, keeping them in check, and she wasn't about to forget the fact that Seth had locked her brother up and refused to listen to reason even while her heart was being yanked to pieces.

And it wasn't only Trey's arrest that caused her such intense grief, but also the loss of their relationship. Shattered trust, by the one man she'd once thought would always be there for her.

She was wrong.

A hard lesson to learn, but one she wouldn't forget.

Frustrated, she yanked on the car door handle and slid behind the wheel. As she started to pull the door shut, Seth stopped the door with his hand. "I'll follow you to the condo."

As much she wanted to get away from this man, she didn't bother to argue. Not like he'd listen anyway. She nodded, turned the ignition and finally breathed.

Fifteen minutes later, Seth pulled into the Beaver Creek condo complex and parked in the spot beside Paige.

As he climbed out of his truck, he could tell by Paige's heated glance that she wasn't thrilled with him being there. Which under normal circumstances might have deterred him from hanging around, but life in Boone was anything but normal these days. And he planned to keep an eye on her until he knew she was out of danger.

Awkward or not, she'd better get used to it.

Paige popped open her umbrella against the light drizzle and started toward the back of her rented car. "Seth, I appreciate your help tonight, but I've wasted enough of your time. I'll just call security and they can escort me to the condo."

"I'm already here." Seth flipped up the collar on his jacket and pocketed his keys. "Just lead the way and I'll make sure you get in safe."

Thunder rumbled in the distance and a frigid breeze kicked up, sending fall leaves skittering along their path as they crossed the parking lot and walked down the brick sidewalk to the front of the condo building.

An awkward silence passed between them as they headed up the wood steps to the third floor. A slight breeze drifted on the cold night air and intensified the uneasiness stirring a pit in Seth's gut. Heightened further by the cool distance Paige kept between them. Not only was she physically several steps ahead of him, emotionally they were light-years apart.

He remembered a day when Paige would have handed him the umbrella and sidled up beside him, staying close and protected from the storm. An awkward moment never existed between them before Trey's arrest. Now, every passing moment they were together was awkward.

Conflicting emotions roiled through him, colliding with each other as he was tempted to sit Paige down and talk through their differences. But he knew if he did, she'd be even more frustrated with him. She was so focused on helping her brother, the last thing she worried about was their unresolved issues. Then again, maybe he was the only one still struggling with how things had ended between them.

Something he needed to fix. Time to get a life. Move on like Paige apparently had.

Okay, enough. Stow the emotional nonsense, Garrison. He ordered himself to get a grip, afraid that if he relaxed his guard he'd be pedaling backward to a place he didn't want to be—falling back in love with Paige Becker.

His relationship with her was way beyond over. He knew that without a doubt. Too bad his rational mind and his heart didn't always see eye to eye—he cared about Paige, even if the feeling wasn't mutual.

Still, annoyance burned in his gut that she put so much energy into avoiding him. Even now.

An old saying of his mother's rolled through his head, and never had it been so fitting. *If you have an issue, come up with a solution.* So, he guessed it was up to him to put a stop to what was annoying him.

Seth leaped up the stairs two at a time and caught up with Paige just as she stepped onto the third-floor landing. "Tie," he huffed, pretending to be out of breath.

Paige jerked to a stop, her eyes wide as her face scrunched in question. "Tie?" She lowered her umbrella.

"You appeared to be racing, and I caught up." He followed with a wink and a sly grin. "So, *tie*." He pumped his right arm in feigned celebration.

Amusement flashed across Paige's green gaze, glittering beneath the overhead lighting in the walkway. Then she laughed, a genuine sound that warmed Seth's heart and eased some of the tension hanging between them.

"Sorry. I didn't mean to get ahead of you. I just didn't want to poke out an eye with my umbrella."

Yeah, right. He nodded. "Good to hear, because I thought you might be trying to avoid me."

The amusement in her gaze faded, replaced by a shadowy look of chagrin, bearing witness to her true feelings. She stuffed her umbrella in her bag. "Honestly, Seth, I appreciate you taking the time to come with me here and walk me to the condo. I'm just exhausted and not thinking clearly. Actually, I'm looking forward to getting home and relaxing."

Him, too. Although relaxing probably wasn't on his agenda for a while. Not until he knew Paige was safe and sound in another county. "Guess we better get you inside, then."

They headed to the condo, the clanking of their heels echoing off the wooden decking as they made their way to the last unit on the left. Seth waited as Paige dug out the key. "Thanks again, Seth," she said, inserting the key in the lock.

She jiggled the doorknob. "This door always sticks." Leaning a shoulder against it, she added more pressure and gave it a push. And as she did, Seth heard a sharp crack.

It sounded like wood splintering. Taking a step back, he looked up. Like the snap of a dead tree limb or—

"Watch out!"

"What's wro—" Paige whirled back, but before she could finish, Seth grabbed onto her and pushed her through the doorway. He hit the ground with a thud, taking Paige with him.

Heart thundering, Seth froze, keeping Paige in his protective hold. It took only a moment more before another sharp fracturing noise split the air; a second later, a large chunk of cedar siding, ripped clean from the side of the building, dropped and swung like a sickle across the doorway, then crashed with an earsplitting *thwack* onto the decking.

"How did that happen?" Paige whispered, fear, coupled with the weight of Seth shielding her body, robbing her breath.

"Good question." Seth's voice held a quivery edge. Combined with the way his heart pounded against hers, she could tell he was as unnerved as she was. "Are you okay?"

"Yes, I think so." She managed a small nod, her heart tripping in her chest.

"Good." He shifted his body away from hers and got to his feet. A sudden coolness prickled her skin, replacing the warmth and comfort of being safe in his arms. An unexplained reaction she wouldn't bother rationalizing at the moment. Then Seth grabbed her hand and helped her up. "Stay put," he said as he pulled out his cell phone, turning it on flashlight mode.

Nausea rolled in Paige's stomach, and her quaking legs threatened to buckle. Taking a step, she leaned heavily against a wood column in the entryway, pressing a hand to her chest. Was this another intentional attack on her life?

She swallowed hard, her throat and mouth suddenly dry as she watched Seth move through the doorway and out the front door. Pitching his flashlight to shine over the wooden threshold, he shook his head with a groan. "Unbelievable. It looks like the only area of damaged siding is just above your front door."

Terror sent tingles of dread shooting through her extremities. He'd just confirmed her worst fear.

An hour and a half later, Paige strode into the Watauga County Sheriff's Department Criminal Investigation Bureau. She walked alongside Seth as they continued down the corridor, shoulders pulled back, feigning nonchalance as if she didn't mind being there. When in truth, she hated the idea.

They stopped outside the evidence processing office, and as Seth leaned against the door frame asking the officer a couple questions, Paige waited a few steps away, trying to adjust to finding herself back in a place reeking with memories of her brother's arrest. Even ten months wasn't long enough to erase the oppressive feelings of déjà vu.

Taking a breath, she looked past Seth to the small waiting room, just beyond a set of double glass doors, where a young woman sat, probably waiting for information on a loved one. A place Paige clearly remembered. She fought back a shiver as her déjà vu moment hit stronger.

Suddenly hot, Paige tugged off her scarf. Seth didn't think it was a good idea for her to stay alone in the condo until after the maintenance crew for Beaver Creek finished inspecting the area of damage over the door. Although she readily agreed, she was now wishing she had just opted to bolt the door shut and wait until morning for the report of their findings.

"Paige Becker."

Paige's heartbeat jumped into a frantic rhythm as she looked up and found Ted Hanson approaching, a broad smile stretching his full lips. "Hey, I don't think I've seen you since you've been back in town."

Which was fine with her. Paige sidled closer to the floor-to-ceiling bookshelf on her left, wishing to just blend into the woodwork. Outside of being Seth's best friend,

Ted had also been one of the detectives on her brother's investigation. "Hi, Ted." She kept her voice cordial.

He stopped right in front of her and lifted a bushy eyebrow at her. "I hope everything's been going okay with you?"

Paige's stomach dropped at the question. Going okay? Was she the only one who remembered her brother was sitting in jail waiting to be tried for murder? Or did people expect someone in her situation to just bounce back to normal and get on with life after the tragic event of her brother's arrest?

If the latter was true, she was still a long way from feeling normal. But she spared him that thought and instead forced a tight smile. "I'm alive." And not in jail. Actually, now that she thought about it, she was better than okay.

Ted's deep chuckle exploded from his chest, warming her despite the heavy burden lingering in her own. "Good, I'm glad."

A sturdy hand squeezed her shoulder, and Paige flinched. Swiveling around, she locked eyes with Seth.

"Hey, I'm waiting for a call back from Brett, and while we're here I'd like to check on a couple other things. I thought you might like to wait in my office."

Was he kidding? *Hallelujah!* "Sure, I'd like to do that."

Paige hadn't so much as turned around when she heard Seth start to fill Ted in on her near miss, as he saw it, at the condo unit. By the time they left the condo, she had recounted the story at least a dozen times to the maintenance supervisor and his crew. The whole ordeal had left her exhausted, and she had no energy to relive that conversation again.

Paige ducked into Seth's office, relieved to be finally out of earshot of any more speculation about the attempts on her life. She only wished they could figure out who wanted her dead.

Slumping into one of the black vinyl chairs across from Seth's desk, she closed her eyes. *Finally, a moment of peace.* She drew in a deep breath and said a quick prayer, grateful that God was watching over her.

She almost found it amusing when she thought about how her life used to be. Ordinary. Average. Even boring at times. What she wouldn't give for a little *ordinary.* Because what her life consisted of now—constantly looking over her shoulder while she tried to unearth evidence with nothing more to go on than a hunch—was really getting old. And dangerous.

And there didn't seem to be an end in sight.

Paige sighed, her moment of peace scrubbed away by that harsh reality.

Opening her eyes, she straightened, tension rippling through her shoulder blades. And in the midst of all the chaos, Seth had been there to help. The parking deck. The courthouse. And now Tessa's condo. She shook her head, trying to take it all in. Despite the hard feelings between them, she was grateful that he'd been there tonight. His navy SEAL training and ardent detective instincts probably saved her life.

Yet the very idea of having to count on Seth during the rest of her stay twisted her stomach into a hard, painful knot. Paige took a deep, steadying breath, trying to fight the guilt eating at her.

She knew she probably should apologize to Seth for requesting to have him removed from her case, but even as guilt pricked her, she knew it was the right thing to do. The reality was, her onetime confidant was now her number one adversary in her quest to clear her brother's name.

Well…outside of the creep that was trying to kill her.

A chill prickled her arms, and she rubbed her hands over them. Still, it touched her heart to know that somewhere deep down Seth still cared about her. He wanted her safe.

Which meant he wanted her gone. Out of Boone.

She breathed deep, trying to curb her disappointment. Clearly their agendas didn't jibe, and it was that misguided attempt of his to keep her safe that only reconfirmed that having him on her case would be a mistake. Ten long months and nothing had changed—not his feelings about her brother or her.

She'd left town and hadn't looked back, and Seth didn't seem to mind in the least.

Swallowing a sigh, Paige pushed all those unproductive thoughts out of her mind.

She shifted more comfortably in the chair and crossed her arms as seconds ticked by in slow motion. Time she didn't have to waste. She glanced at the clock on the wall and the pendulum swaying lazily back and forth as silence stretched across the room. The clock, a rustic old-world design, was the one she'd given to Seth for his birthday last year. She'd laughed when he told her where he was going to hang it. He said having it in his office would keep him prompt for their dates. But there was more than a bit of irony in that statement, because Seth was the definition of prompt.

Seth took everything in his life seriously. A tough, brave and dedicated detective. Ethical. Caring. A master of multitasking. Brilliant in every way, yet so wrong about her brother. She shook her head.

Okay. Enough of that. Sucking in a deep breath, Paige got to her feet and went to the window. Lightning flashed. Thunder rumbled in the distance. Another stormy night.

Pitch-black. No stars or moon to brighten up the obsidian gloom or quell the even darker fears inside her heart.

"Paige."

She spun around from the window as Brett's deep voice rumbled through the room. She also had an appreciation for him; he was never more than a phone call away. Even if it was his day off. "Brett, thanks for coming."

Brett stepped deeper into the room, his pale blue eyes shadowed. "Not a problem. How are you doing?"

Seth followed in close on his heels. He stepped around Brett and, without so much as a glance in Paige's direction, went straight to his desk and turned on his laptop.

Her gaze returned to Brett. She gave a small shrug. "I've had better days."

A rare smile tipped Brett's thin lips. "I'd like to think so."

And she was ready to call this day done. "Surely, the maintenance workers are finished by now. Because I'm ready to get out of here."

"Actually—" Brett crossed his arms over his chest. "—I just spoke to Jack, the maintenance crew chief at Beaver Creek, and he said they are finished."

"And?" She held her breath.

Brett gave an offhand shrug. "From what they found, it doesn't appear foul play was involved."

Immediately the stress in her shoulders started to evaporate, and for the first time since she'd arrived in Boone, she felt a genuine smile tug at her lips. Finally, good news amid a myriad of other concerns. "So, a close call," she said, splaying a hand against her chest. "But no intentional threat to my life. Wonderful."

"That's how it appears." Brett sounded confident. "The complex got hit pretty hard during the recent storm. Several of the buildings had serious damage. The area of siding over your door has probably been hanging on by a thread since then."

As Paige listened to Brett's explanation, the memory of the violent storm stirred vividly in her mind. The maintenance crew's rationale made perfect sense.

Feeling relieved, she grabbed her handbag and jacket from the chair, suddenly feeling more antsy about getting out of there. "Thanks for the information. I feel much better."

"I wouldn't be too quick to make light of what happened tonight," Seth interjected, glancing up from his computer. "Another possibility you may consider is that the recent storm and all its damage could give a person with an agenda to kill a perfect opportunity to stage an accident. No questions asked. And no one would be the wiser."

Brett gave Seth a scathing look, clearly not liking his hypothesis. And Paige agreed with him. Storm damage was a common phenomenon. But Seth could be a skeptic, so she wasn't surprised by his assumption, even if it was a stretch for her own overactive imagination.

"Paige, I think for now we should just go with the obvious." Brett flashed her a decisive look.

"All right," she said, slightly under her breath. She felt awkward taking sides, but Brett was the detective running her investigation.

"Then I guess we're done for now." Brett fished his keys out of his coat pocket and turned toward the door. "If you'd like a lift home, I'll be going right by your place."

Perfect. She brightened a bit. She'd already put Seth through enough for one day. But her heart tightened as Seth pushed his chair back and stood. A muscle ticked in his jaw, the expression that overtook him whenever he was deeply concerned or annoyed. At the moment, she'd say both probably applied. He obviously didn't buy the maintenance crew's conclusion, not wanting to settle for such a simple explanation. Brett, on the other hand, was more black-and-white. Polar opposites. Paige wasn't sure whether to further acknowledge Seth's concerns or leave it alone.

"Paige, ready?" Brett waited at the door.

Okay. *Leave it alone.*

"Yes." She slipped on her coat and slung her purse strap over her shoulder. "I'm ready."

As Seth grabbed his jacket from the back of a chair and wrestled it on, he threw a testy glance at Brett before meeting Paige's gaze. "Stay safe. Call if you need anything."

She nodded and followed Brett out the door. A fist of fresh grief squeezed her heart. She needed plenty, but unfortunately, nothing that involved Seth Garrison.

FIVE

Two o'clock in the morning and Seth couldn't sleep. Instead he was up, pacing tirelessly back and forth in the living room of his home, a rustic cabin located on a twenty-acre wooded parcel that at one time he'd hoped to share with Paige. *Paige*. The woman he couldn't get out of his head.

Stubborn. Naive. Beautiful. Willing to risk her life on a hunch that her brother was innocent. A *maybe* that all the evidence pointing to him had been tampered with and the real murderer was still out there.

A ludicrous endeavor, Seth's rational mind shouted, even as a small, distal part of his brain whispered, *What if Paige is right?*

Whoa. Seth halted his march, his spine snapping taut. Where had that thought come from? He'd been Trey's arresting officer. He'd been objective. Considered every angle. Scrutinized every ounce of evidence.

The case was airtight. Seth rubbed his head as if to solidify those facts. Still, a sliver of skepticism lingered. Seth shook it away and picked up his march, paced to the family room, turned around and went back to the kitchen, chalking up any doubt in his mind to exhaustion.

Yep. His brain was fried.

But no matter if he harbored skepticism about Trey's guilt, Seth carried no doubt that someone out there wanted Paige dead. A harsh reality that kept him on edge.

And with that reality came questions, concerns that kept his mind reeling as he tried to figure out what could be driving her attacker. Revenge? Or was there something deeper, a score they'd yet to consider?

Whatever the motive, her pursuer was creative and persistent. That fact burned like fire in his gut.

And the closer they got to Trey's trial, the more desperate Paige would be to find evidence to help him, and her perpetrator equally desperate to get to her.

Exasperation tightened Seth's chest as fear for Paige's safety shot to the red zone.

Paige was a smart woman, and yet, no matter the evidence spotlighting her brother's guilt or the dangerous situations she'd found herself in since she'd been in Boone, she couldn't be convinced to take a step back and allow Trey's future to rest with the court.

And with that stubborn spirit, it was only a matter of time before she ended up getting hurt. Or worse.

The need to protect her niggled deep in Seth's gut, but he tamped it down, reminding himself that Paige was an independent woman and no longer part of his life. She could do what she wanted to do.

That rationale lasted about a split second before concern for Paige bubbled back up.

And the worst part—there was nothing he could do about it.

Huffing a sigh, Seth made a sharp right toward the window, stepping over a pile of wood trim left over from his ongoing renovation. A project he'd planned to work on during his time off over the next few days.

An idea he'd given up on for the time being. Along

with getting any sleep. Every time his head hit the pillow, his brain flipped into overdrive. Trying to figure out the details of Paige's case.

Who was after Paige? And why?

Seth halted his steps and peered out the window. Darkness. Not even the moon in the sky. A sharp wind blew, trees creaked and whined, leaves rustled. As tumultuous outside as the turmoil brewing inside him.

Paige wasn't going to budge. No matter what got in her way. And in Seth's opinion, Brett being on her case wasn't helping things. He was looking at things way too objectively. Something Seth always strove to do also, but with Paige's safety on the line, he wished Brett would be a little more proactive.

Because right now, Seth couldn't shake his concern or erase the reality that someone had it out for Paige.

Sighing a long breath, Seth wheeled around and headed to the living room. He grabbed his work laptop. Fretting was unproductive and only ramped up his concern. With sleep not on his agenda, he might as well do a little investigating himself.

He nudged his old hound, Laser, from his recliner and sat down. Then, positioning his laptop on the coffee table, he signed in to his work account and into the department's resource website. He punched Gentry Cramer's name into the browser window, and dozens of articles linked to him popped on the screen. Local news pieces, criminal background information, even obituary notices for his sister and father in which he was listed as a family member.

Seth clicked on one link after another and read through articles depicting a variety of things, from Gentry's glowing community service endeavors to his outspoken views about his sister's murder. Seth also verified his criminal history. Clean. Not even a speeding ticket. The guy was a model citizen, brother and son.

Gentry had never been a suspect in the case. Even though Gentry had zeroed in on Trey from the get-go, confident he'd killed Madison, that hadn't raised red flags. With all the evidence they had, he wasn't alone.

But with the recent threats on Paige's life, Seth couldn't help but wonder if Gentry's anger toward Trey had pushed him to take revenge. And Paige being back in Boone offered a perfect opportunity to do so.

A fine hypothesis. Now all he needed was evidence to prove it. And at the same time keep Paige out of his way.

Seth blew out a frustrated breath and continued his search, reading every article that scrolled across the screen that mentioned the name Gentry Cramer. And there was no shortage of them. The man was active in the community. An expert in antiques and the art world. He'd even started a foundation in honor of his sister.

Seth found nothing too noteworthy until an article about Frank Cramer, Madison and Gentry's father, popped up on the screen. Sitting up straighter, Seth took a moment to skim through it.

Frank had been killed by a drunk driver. The driver, a prominent man from a neighboring county, survived but later served time for Cramer's death.

Seth settled back in his leather recliner, fingers steepled, pressed against his lip, wondering if the Cramers had been awarded a financial settlement after Frank's death. Seth had always heard stories that at the time of the accident, the community came together and rallied around the family. Seth had assumed their help was monetary, but maybe the Cramers didn't need financial help.

Seth closed his laptop with a snap. Kicking back in the recliner, he crossed his arms and let those thoughts sink in. Maybe there was more than a broken heart at stake for Trey when he and Madison split—one more reason that might have driven him to kill his wife?

The next morning Paige was up and out of the condo before seven and, after what seemed like a lifetime, finally arrived at her destination. She looked over both shoulders and then started up the brick walkway to a small clapboard bungalow on Elm Street. Amy Miles's home. She hated to be paranoid, but she was aware of the fact that someone was keeping close tabs on her. And she wasn't taking any chances. For her sake and Amy's. And as much as she hated to drag Amy into this mess, she needed her help.

Taking a deep breath, she marched up to the porch, then up several steps. Gnawing the inside of her lip, Paige took another quick look over her shoulder, running her eyes up and down the street. So far, so good. No cars on the road. No one lurking around. She breathed a little easier.

She'd ditched her car at Paulie's Restaurant on Main Street and jumped on the Appalcart, the city's public bus. After two hours, four bus transfers and several different not so scenic routes around town, she finally got off at Appalachian Drive and walked the final two blocks to Elm Street.

Hopefully, if someone had been on her tail, they were long lost by now.

She said a little prayer reiterating that concern. In the four days since she'd arrived in Boone, she'd met one obstacle after another. But today everything seemed to be falling into place.

After a long night of debating, she'd gotten up, and before she lost her nerve, she'd grabbed her cell phone and dialed Cramer's Antiques. She'd taken a huge risk, especially if Gentry happened to answer the phone. She would likely be looking at harassment to go along with the trespassing charge she'd already been slapped with.

But fortunately her risk had paid off. Sarah, another clerk from the shop, had answered the phone and informed her that Amy had called in sick and wouldn't be in. And that tidbit of information afforded Paige an opportunity to talk to Amy alone, away from the watchful eye of her boss, Gentry Cramer.

And finally Paige was here, ready and hopeful.

Paige felt for her cell phone in her pocket. Still there. She'd spent the majority of her bus ride making notes on discussion topics and questions for Amy. As long as she was here, she wanted to find out all she could.

That is, if Amy would even agree to talk to her.

Her anxiety ratcheted up a notch. *Okay, enough.* Paige drew in a deep breath. *Let's get this over with.* She gave her phone a quick squeeze and then pulled out her hand and tapped on the storm door.

The sun was shining. An unseasonably warm sixty-five degrees. A beautiful October morning. Everything was going to be fine, she reassured herself.

A long minute ticked by, then two. Paige held her breath, then blew it out hard when no one came to the door.

Paige took a step back, glanced around for a doorbell. There wasn't one. She knocked again. Waited. Said a quick prayer.

Still no answer.

With hope waning, Paige headed back down the porch steps and along the brick sidewalk to the right side of the house, where a blue sedan was parked beneath an attached metal carport.

As she stood there a moment assessing the situation, she heard the blast of a whistle from inside the house.

Paige jumped, nerves jangled. The whistle grew louder, shrill. *A teakettle.* Paige relaxed a little. Amy must be home.

In the driveway, she circled around the back of the car, and as she reached the steps leading to the enclosed breezeway, she noticed that the door stood ajar. Paige stopped in her tracks.

The whistling continued. Loud and intense. How could someone in the house miss that?

A shiver danced along Paige's spine. She shook it off. Amy had probably stepped out for a moment. Paige turned and scanned the front yard. No sign of Amy or anyone.

Paige continued to the door, a knot in her stomach. Hopefully, Amy was okay. Then she remembered how when her brother was young he could sleep through almost anything. That possibility calmed her some.

She knocked once. "Hello? Amy?" Then tried again louder when her knock went unanswered.

Paige's stomach clenched with nerves. No response again. No sound, except for the squealing kettle.

Paige pulled open the screen door and stepped inside. The warm scent of chicken soup—one of her favorite homespun remedies for cold and flu—filled the air.

"Amy?" Paige called again from the breezeway.

Silence. Uneasiness slithered up and down her spine. Something didn't feel right.

Swallowing hard, Paige tried to squelch the fear bubbling inside her as she followed the smell and deafening whistle down a short hallway, past an empty bedroom and a bathroom on the right.

A little farther down the hall, an opening to the left

proved to be the kitchen. She stepped in and glanced around. Empty also, except for the bubbling pot on the stove and the screaming kettle. She turned off the stove and slid the kettle to another burner. Despite Paige's iron-clad grip on her composure, her knees went a little wobbly as she stepped out of the kitchen and into the next room.

The lights were off and the blinds closed. In the dimness of the living room, her eye caught something—no, *someone*—lying on the carpet beside the sofa. Heart rattling, she fumbled with the light switch on the wall. The yellow glow of lamplight scattered the darkness and confirmed what her heart already knew. A body.

No! Paige's mind screamed, horror stealing her breath. She couldn't scream. Couldn't breathe. Every muscle numbed. Frozen from disbelief as her world slowed. Came to halt.

"Amy," Paige finally managed to grind out, blinking against the wash of hot tears stinging her eyes.

No answer came. Only silence. Cold. Dead. Silence.

Panic ricocheted through Paige. She grabbed the wall to keep from toppling over, nausea roiling in her stomach, bile clawing its way up her throat. Amy Miles was dead. Lying on the floor, a bloody gash on the side of her head.

The room started to close in on Paige as panic gave way to terror. Suddenly, she could feel the killer's presence. Was he still here? Waiting for her?

Heart pounding, Paige turned and darted out of the room. She ran down the hall, slammed open the breezeway door and catapulted herself down the four steps to the carport. As she sprinted around the parked car, her feet stumbled over each other. She landed hard, dirt and gravel digging into her palms and knees as she skidded across the concrete. Picking herself up, she kept going, racing down the driveway and to the curb.

Yanking the cell phone from her pocket, she collapsed against the streetlight, hot tears biting her eyes. She blinked them back, and with fingers trembling, managed to punch in the digits. Nine-one-one.

Clutching the phone to her ear, she spoke some of the hardest words she could ever imagine over the lump of emotion clogging her throat. "I think there's been a murder…"

Long desperate moments chugged by as shock tightened around Paige like a noose, numbing every synapse, every fiber of her being. Sirens blared, boots thudded, stretchers clanked, followed by a cacophony of panicked voices.

Chaos.

Uniformed professionals. First responders. Police. Paramedics. An army of rescuers flooded the area. But there was nothing anyone could do to change reality.

Amy Miles was dead.

"Paige" came a voice from behind her. The deep, resonant sound brought both comfort and unease. She took a deep breath, trying to dispel the irrational leap in her heart rate at just having Seth near.

Straightening on shaky legs, Paige turned to face him. "Are you okay?" A deep sadness was so evident in the taut lines of his face. "I got a call from Ted. He told me Amy Miles was dead."

At just hearing those words, hot tears threatened to spill. Paige blinked and nodded. "Yes. Amy is dead." The words stung, singeing her already parched throat, and Seth just stood there shaking his head.

"Ted said it looked like she died of a blunt trauma," he

said after a moment. "There was blood on the end table as if she fell and hit her head."

Paige glared at him, shock setting in. "They think it was an accident?"

He shook his head. "It may have been set up to look like an accident, but from the deep gash in her head and where the wound was located, the team suspects foul play."

Good. She swallowed, hating she felt better knowing the detectives suspected Amy had been murdered.

He laid a gentle hand on her shoulder. "I'm sorry you've gotten pulled into this."

"Well, I'm sorry that Amy had to die." Paige stepped out of his grasp, annoyed at the warmth sizzling through her at his simple touch. "Her deranged killer has to be the same person who killed Madison. And he's this close—" she separated her finger and thumb an inch apart "—to getting away with murder. If someone doesn't stop him, more people are going to die." *Maybe even me.*

Seth folded his arms, the warmth in his gaze lingering. "This is a terrible tragedy and terribly emotional for you. But let's not jump to those conclusions yet."

Paige looked away. She didn't want his empathy or his rationale, she wanted this nightmare to stop. She swallowed hard, trying to keep it together. "Madison's dead. Amy's dead. Somebody wants me dead. What's it going to take, Seth, for you to finally believe Madison's killer is still out there?"

"Paige—"

"No, wait. I know what you're going to say." She looked back at him and shot up her hand. "Evidence. You need evidence." She gestured at the house behind her. "Isn't this enough? Amy knew or suspected something, and now she's dead."

"Paige." The compassion in Seth's voice did nothing to quell the panic rioting through her insides. "Forensics detectives are on the scene collecting evidence. We'll know more in the next couple days. In the meantime, please be patient."

"Patient?" Paige's voice sharpened. "It's not easy being patient when my brother is stuck in jail and ready to face charges for a crime he didn't commit. And now Amy Miles, the one person who shed the slightest doubt on his guilt, is dead." She swiped back frustrated tears now streaming from her eyes.

Not to mention she was still trying to convince everyone her brother was innocent while a nameless madman had her on his hit list. Making patience pretty much impossible.

A deputy officer joined them. Turning his back to her, he spoke only to Seth, keeping his voice low enough that Paige couldn't hear what he was saying as he gestured across the yard to where other detectives and the chief stood talking.

"Paige, I'll be right back." Seth touched her arm, and Paige took a deep breath. She almost felt guilty how frustrated she was with him. She knew he only wanted to help, to keep her safe, but she also knew how he planned to accomplish those goals. For her to leave town. And with what happened today, she honestly concurred.

As Seth crossed the grass, Paige sank against the streetlight again. An icy chill settled over her, and she hugged her arms to her chest. Angrily, she blew the hair from her eyes. How could something like this have happened?

Paige stared at the empty house. Red brick. Neat and clean. Manicured bushes. Pots of fall flowers on the stoop. Amy's home.

Now a crime scene.

A river of emotions churned in her stomach at the raw truth. Tears came then, scalding hot, blurring her vision. She swallowed hard, slammed her eyes shut. *God, help me. I am at such a loss. Every direction I take turns tragic.* And now someone else was dead.

"Paige, how are you doing?"

Paige snapped her eyes open and found Brett standing in front of her, anguish and disbelief stamped on his face. "Things are getting pretty crazy around here," he said, shaking his head.

She nodded, gathering her scattered emotions. "I feel responsible, Brett. If I hadn't stopped by the Cramers' shop yesterday, Amy would probably still be alive."

Brett shrugged as if he agreed with what she'd said, upping Paige's anxiety. She dragged her bottom lip between her teeth. She could feel the tears building again.

Brett must have sensed her despair because his eyes turned soft and a sober expression claimed his face. His mouth opened as he started to say something, but then it closed as Seth stepped up beside him.

"Paige, this isn't your doing," Seth interjected without reserve. "You can't take responsibility for what someone else has done."

She nodded, feeling a smidge better. But the guilt corkscrewing through her midsection was hard to convince.

"It is a terrible loss," Brett said, his face in its usual taut lines, his gaze guarded again. "But it's certainly not your fault." As he echoed Seth's sentiments, a deeper concern etched into his features.

As Paige gazed at him, she was reminded of Seth's face the day he showed up to deliver the news of Madison's death. She had never seen him so distraught, having to tell her not only about Trey's arrest but also that he'd been charged with murder.

Her heart squeezed tight. Tragedies like this could never be easy. Appreciation surged for the men and women who dealt with murder and death on a regular basis as part of their job. *Lord, forgive me for not seeing their value until now.*

"But don't worry, Paige." Brett's words snapped her back. He offered her his handkerchief. "We'll dive into this full force and get to the bottom of who's responsible for Amy's murder."

Thank You, God. She nodded, taking his offering. She blotted her eyes.

"But," he continued, "everyone on the investigative team agrees that you're not safe here in Boone. The best thing for you to do is leave and let us do our job."

Paige's fingers balled into a fist around the hankie. She wasn't going anywhere. Why didn't they get it? The sharp trill of her cell phone put that question on hold. She yanked it out. All eyes stayed glued on her.

When she checked the caller ID, hope soared. It was Chet Andrews, Trey's lead attorney. Hopefully, he had some kind of good news. He spoke quickly, succinctly. But the news that he had to share was of the worst kind.

Paige disconnected the call with shaky hands. Taking a deep breath, she slowly lifted her gaze to meet Seth's. "The court date for Trey's murder trial has been moved."

Seth's brown eyes squinted beneath furrowed brows. "So it's no longer scheduled for the seventeenth of October?"

Paige barely found the energy to wag her head no, hardly believing what she'd just heard. "Due to a scheduling conflict at the courthouse, it's been moved up to next Wednesday, the tenth." One week away.

* * *

"Hey, Ted, let me have a look at that."

In the interrogation room, Seth edged past Brett and headed toward the door where Ted stood holding the preliminary autopsy report for Amy Miles.

"It shows blunt force trauma to the head. Extensive contusions on arms and abdomen. Manner of death is listed as homicide." Ted summarized as Seth skimmed the report.

"Thanks, Ted." The report confirmed what they'd already suspected. And there was no forced entry, so the killer knew Amy. Someone who thought Amy knew something about his involvement in Paige's attacks? One person came to mind—Gentry.

Turning around, he handed the report to Brett, who was standing behind him looking over his shoulder. "Here you go." Brett took it, reciprocating with an annoyed look.

Brett made no bones about his feelings on Seth being there. Which didn't bother Seth in the least. His only concern right now was keeping an eye on Paige, whether Brett liked it or not.

"So how's Paige taking all this?" Ted asked, propping a shoulder against the doorjamb.

"She's distraught, still trying to process everything," Seth said.

"It's a lot to process," Ted said. "Finding a dead body is pretty upsetting. And from the report, it sounds like she didn't miss the killer by much."

"No, she didn't. The door was open and a teakettle squealing. Amy hadn't been dead long." Another close call. Seth ground his teeth, wishing Paige would use this as a wakeup call for her safety. "She's in the lobby waiting. Stop by and say hello." Hopefully, she was still there.

He hated the idea of her being out on the streets of Boone alone at the moment.

Ted nodded. "I might just do that," he said, crossing his arms. "So, have any other witnesses come forward?"

"Not yet." Seth shook his head, draping his sturdy frame against the edge of the table. "We spoke to several people in the neighborhood, and so far no one's admitted to hearing or seeing anything. Other than the statement from Paige, we've got nothing."

"How about physical evidence?"

Seth shook his head again. "Nope, batting zero there also. No signs of forced entry. No murder weapon. Right now, forensics is our only hope." Totally opposite of Madison's murder, where evidence was ready and waiting for them.

Ted inched up his brow, whistling. "Buddy, you do have your work cut out for you—"

"Yes, I do," Brett interrupted with a scowl. He stepped around Seth and eyed Ted directly. "We still have officers at the scene. If there's any evidence out there, I'm confident they'll find it."

"I'm sure they will." Ted exchanged a glance with Seth, shooting him a knowing grin. "I'll let you guys get back to work."

"Thanks, Ted," Seth said.

Brett turned his glare on Seth. "I know Mullins wants you here, but keep in mind that I'm the lead detective on this case and Paige's." He pointed an accusing finger at Seth. "And you're supposed to be still on vacation, so I'd appreciate it if you—" Brett's cell phone started to ring, blotting out the rest of his request. Sighing, he reached for his phone in his jacket and shoved it at his ear. "Ralston here."

Good. Seth didn't need to hear more. He got Brett's

drift, but it stuck in his craw that Brett seemed more concerned about his place on the case than Paige's safety. Because if safety came first, he'd be recruiting more officers to brainstorm with. Help was help, and he was going to need it.

Seth's vacation had in reality ended the moment he realized Paige was back in town. Even if Paige didn't want his help, he was back on the job and planned to help crack her case. He folded his arms and waited as Brett finished his call, attentively nodding as he spoke. "...Thank you, we're ready for him."

Showtime. Seth settled into a metal folding chair at the scarred wood table and waited for Gentry Cramer to be brought in. He'd been asked by the investigative team to voluntarily come in for questioning. Seth was actually surprised by Gentry's easy acceptance. He was either trying to be proactive and keep his name out of this mess or he understood it was better to cooperate now on his own than risk being forced to.

Either way, it didn't matter. Gentry hadn't quite jumped to suspect status, but after his run-in with Paige yesterday and now Amy's murder today, he was officially a person of interest. And cooperating was to his advantage.

By the time the uniformed officer opened the door and escorted Gentry in, Brett had already stood up to greet them. "Mr. Cramer, thank you for agreeing to come in. Please take a seat and we'll get started." He gestured toward the table where Seth was already seated, getting straight to business.

Seth liked that about Brett. Plainspoken. He didn't beat around the bush. For interrogation tactics it played in his favor. Otherwise, not so much.

Standing opposite the one-way mirror, Gentry didn't

acknowledge Brett's request. Instead his gaze skipped
around the dim room—the bare walls, mounted cameras,
lone table illuminated by a single beam of light, where
his gaze stopped.

Seth hadn't seen Gentry since the day of Madison's
death when he showed up at the crime scene demand-
ing answers. And Gentry didn't look any less frustrated
now than he did then.

"Garrison, I should have known you'd be here," Gentry barked, fixing him with a caustic stare. "Like her
brother, Paige must have you, too, wrapped around her
finger. Too bad you can't keep that woman of yours under
control."

Seth shifted back in the chair. Although the inference
irked him, he wasn't about to go head-to-head with Gentry. Especially over something that wasn't true. He wasn't
wrapped around anyone's finger, and Paige was hardly
out of control. Stubborn? Yes. Dedicated? To a fault. She
was a sister fighting for her brother's life.

Whoa.

Seth bit back a growl and immediately flushed those
thoughts. Here he was defending Paige—to himself.

Seth rolled his shoulders against the tension coiling
through them. Nonetheless, he was glad the chief pulled
him back on the case that morning. Being the arresting
officer for Trey Becker earned him a place at the table.
Things had gotten dangerous in Boone, and Seth had the
most knowledge about Trey Becker's case. As the dividing line between Paige's case and Madison's murder continued to blur, he'd been charged to help narrow down
a suspect and motive to give the case a definitive focus.
Right now they were grasping at straws.

And the one positive to getting pulled into the fray—
he no longer had to wonder what was going on with

Paige's investigation, even if Brett was not happy that the chief had pulled him into the case.

"Let's get on with it," Gentry said, pulling out a chair and seating himself directly in front of Seth. "I've got things to get to, so this better not take long."

"That depends on you," Seth said, sliding to the edge of his seat. "The more you cooperate, the quicker we get out of here."

"I'm not on trial here, but I'll do my best." Gentry glared at Seth, impatience etched into the lines of his face.

Brett cleared his throat. He stood off to the side, arms folded over his chest, looking like a sentinel ready to pounce if Gentry tried anything.

They should be so fortunate. Seth knew Gentry wasn't about to do anything crazy that would get him arrested. He was just testing the waters, deliberately attempting to try their patience while making it clear that he didn't like having fingers pointed at him.

"I guess we've come full circle, haven't we?" Gentry sat forward, plunking both elbows on the table. "My sister was brutally murdered. Now the murderer's sister comes back to Boone and stumbles into harm's way, and somehow I'm the one being looked at. Amazing."

"*Accused* murderer," Seth corrected and didn't wait for Brett to interject. Instead he followed Gentry's lead and sat forward in his seat. "So, tell me, Gentry. Are we off base with that assumption?"

Gentry glowered, clearly not liking Seth's question. And his insolent expression didn't rate well with Seth. Where was the gregarious gentleman social media raved about? Community activist, model citizen. Apparently a couple of lowly sheriff's department investigators weren't worth his time trying to impress.

"Yes, you are *way* off base." His nostrils flared in anger. "Other than having Miss Becker arrested for trespassing, I haven't had any other interaction with the woman."

Seth leaned closer. "Are you aware Amy Miles died today?"

"Yes." Gentry frowned. "A tragedy."

"It is a tragedy." Seth met his gaze. "We believe foul play was involved."

Gentry stared back, quiet for a moment. "Shocking. I hope you find the culprit."

"We're working on it." Seth scratched beside his nose. "So tell me, Gentry, what kind of interactions have you had with Amy?"

"I don't believe this." Gentry scoffed and flopped back in his seat as heat rose up his neck and flooded his face. "Amy worked for my family since she was a teenager." He stopped, cleared his voice to gather composure. "The loss of Amy is just ripping me apart. She was a close family friend."

Close friend? Paige's description of Amy's demeanor yesterday at the antique mart hovered in Seth's mind. *Nervous. Hesitant.* She kept telling Paige she shouldn't be there. *A fearful employee* seemed a better description. Seth cleared his voice. "How did you and Amy get along?"

His dark brows pulled into a tight frown. "I just told you she was like family."

"Not all families get along."

"Well, we did. We got along just fine." Anger sparked in Gentry's gaze. "I know what you're trying to do, Garrison. Get me to say something that you can misconstrue. But you've got nothing to tie me to Amy's murder or whatever is going on with Paige. I don't even know why you pulled me in here today."

"I understand your frustration," Seth said with a nod. "However, Paige has had her life threatened since she's been in town, and now Amy Miles has been murdered. It is our job to talk to people who've had interaction with both of them, and you're one of those people."

"Yeah, right." Gentry shook his head. "That's just a bunch of cop gibberish for *we ain't got nothing, so let's look at you.*"

Seth chose to ignore the dig and so did Brett. Instead Brett redirected as he stepped closer to the table. "Yesterday you saw Amy Miles talking to Paige. How did you react to that?"

"This is nonsense," Gentry mumbled, straightening up in his seat. "I was irritated, but not at Amy. What upset me is that Paige had the nerve to step foot into my shop. How can she think she'd be welcome after what her brother did to Madison—"

"Hold up there, Gentry." Seth held up his palms, trying to keep a neutral tone. "I want to remind you again that Trey may be facing charges for murder, but he hasn't been convicted."

"Yet." Gentry's jaw flexed and the word hung like a question mark in the air.

Seth shifted in his seat and crossed his arms over his chest, ignoring the little what-if banging through his head: What if they were wrong about Trey? *Nah.* He kicked that thought out and pressed on. That assumption was a long way off. He cleared his throat. "Do you know why Amy would have doubts that Trey killed your sister?"

Gentry's eyes narrowed to an icy glare. "I wouldn't know. She never expressed that opinion to me."

"Does her opinion surprise you?"

Gentry gave a bored shrug. "Amy was a bit of a busy-body. She liked information and didn't mind telling people what they wanted to hear. So who knows what she said or really believed?"

"It seems that something she *believed* got her killed."

"Again, Detective, I wouldn't know," Gentry said, folding his burly arms.

"No thoughts on why someone might have killed her?"

Gentry just sat there, his hard-nosed attitude perfected.

Seth shifted in his seat. "Who did Amy speak to this morning when she called in sick?"

Gentry's look thawed a degree, but his face remained in a frown. "The employees know to leave a voice message for me on the shop phone. I check messages when I get to work around eight. The answering machine showed Amy called at 7:26."

Assuming Gentry was telling the truth, 7:26 gave someone with an agenda to kill plenty of time to get in and out before Paige showed up at the crime scene around ten that morning. *Someone who knew Amy would be home for the day.*

Brett obviously had the same thoughts. He placed his palms on the table and leaned in, forcing Gentry to look at him. "After you received Amy's message, what were you doing the next two and a half hours?"

Gentry's lips flattened to an irritated line. "I went to my mother's house. I work there the days I have conference calls. Our foreign business records are in my late father's office, and there are fewer interruptions."

Brett slipped into the chair beside Seth, eyeing Gentry directly. "Is there someone who can substantiate that?"

"Like someone other than *my mother*?" Gentry answered with a sarcastic snap.

"Anyone that actually saw you there," Brett pointed out drily. "I know your mother has been out of town."

The frown between Gentry's thick brows deepened. He hadn't been expecting that. Neither had Seth, and he straightened up, actually impressed. Brett was more on top of the investigation than he thought.

"I spoke to her housekeeper, Mildred Peck," Brett clarified. "She told me your mother's been staying with her sister for the last six months."

"Yes, she has," Gentry admitted without so much as a chagrined flinch in his expression. "However, I always call her when I'm at her house. Feel free to check the phone records."

"We are talking about two and half hours, Gentry." Seth was losing his patience. "Certainly you weren't on the phone with your mother that long."

"I figured I might need this." Gentry rocked back in the chair, dug into his pocket and pulled out a piece of paper. "I had a Skype conference from eight fifteen until almost ten." He slid the paper across the table. "It's a Skype log from the computer in my father's office. Take a look." He graced Seth with a sardonic look. "Those Asian vendors can be long-winded when they're trying to sell something."

Brett picked up the call log, quickly assessed it and then handed it back to Gentry.

"Thanks." Gentry pocketed the paper. "Now can I get out of here? I have a business to run."

"One more question," Brett said. "Did Amy have any issues with anyone that you know of? Someone in her personal life or a coworker?"

"I wouldn't know." Gentry shrugged. "I stay out of my employees' business at work and otherwise."

Yeah, right. Then how did he know Amy liked to gossip? Seth shook his head.

"Okay." Brett straightened with a sigh. "That's it for now. I'm sure we'll have more questions and be back in touch."

"Actually, I have a question," Seth said calmly, earning him a sharp brow lift from Brett. "After the automobile accident that claimed your father's life several years ago, did your family ever receive a financial settlement?"

Halfway out of the chair, Gentry froze, his backside suspended in midair. "What kind of question is that?" he grunted, an insolent look on his face.

One that obviously hit a nerve. Seth hitched a shoulder. "Just looking for information. We need to consider all angles."

Gentry's eyes narrowed. "Do you really think Madison's murder would have anything to do with our family trust?"

Interesting concept. One Seth planned to explore. He smiled. "Was Trey aware of Madison's share of the trust?"

Gentry's face went placid and he reclaimed his seat. "I'm not sure what Madison told him. We've always kept our finances private. I'm not even sure if Madison knew how much her share was…"

Seth sat back and let him talk, the tension in the room easing as the conversation shifted away from Gentry and toward Trey.

"…I'm usually the one in touch with the executor," Gentry concluded. "When Madison needed money, she'd let me know."

But Gentry knew exactly how much money was in her

trust. Seth's ears perked, and he tucked that little tidbit to the back of his mind. Refraining from commenting further, Seth waited for Brett to interject. He didn't.

"Is that it?" Gentry raised his hands after a moment.

"For now," Seth said. "However, I'd appreciate it if you'd keep your distance from Paige. That way your intentions can't be misconstrued." He fixed Gentry with a hard stare, hoping he caught his drift. His remark was no idle threat, just in case Gentry had any intentions of causing Paige grief—or worse. He'd have to contend with Seth first.

Gentry got to his feet. "No problem. Just tell her to stay away from my shop."

"Thank you, Mr. Cramer. We appreciate your cooperation." Brett pushed back in his chair.

Seth followed suit, adding, "We'll be in touch."

"Seth." Brett caught him on the way out the door. The look of disdain on his face told Seth he was in the hot seat again. Brett kept his voice low and direct. "Why didn't you tell me about the Cramers' family trust?"

Seth lifted a shoulder. "I wasn't sure there was one. Or even if it was relevant."

"But you suspected there was and didn't bother to mention it to me?"

Seth felt his teeth grit. Amy Miles was dead, and Paige's life was in jeopardy. They didn't have time for sore egos. "It just came to mind, Brett. So I asked about it."

"Anything else you suspect but haven't mentioned?" The annoyance in Brett's eyes shone bright. "Because if we have to work together, I don't want any more surprises."

A glance at the hard line of Brett's jaw only reinforced why Seth preferred to work alone. Seth shook his head.

"Nothing I can think of. But if I have an inkling about something, I'll be sure to share it."

Brett jerked a short nod, and Seth drew in a long, narrow breath and walked out the door. *Oh, brother.* He'd only officially rejoined the case a couple hours ago and already conflict was brewing.

SIX

By the time Seth finally stepped back into the lobby, Paige was full of questions about Gentry and what, if any, information they'd garnered from him. She hadn't expected that Gentry would come out and openly admit his guilt, but after her interaction with Gentry yesterday and Amy's untimely death today, surely he had risen to the top of the suspect list. But Seth was frustratingly tight-lipped about their conversation and suspicions of him, saying only, "Gentry was more obstinate than cordial. But he did cooperate."

Detective jargon for *there's nothing you need to know.* Which meant she was left to come up with her own conclusions. And, with all the fear-driven anxiety clawing at her brain, hardly a reliable source of surmising.

Seth gestured toward the upholstered sofa and chairs in the lobby. "Brett's checking with the forensics team for an update on their findings. So if you'd like to have a seat, I have a couple more questions for you."

More questions? Paige's muscles chilled. She'd already spent an hour being grilled about her interactions with Amy and Gentry the day before and her discovery of Amy's body today. She was pretty much talked out. "I've already told you everything I know. Everything I saw—"

"It's okay, Paige." Seth placed his hand on her arm, the warmth of his touch deescalating her panic. "We're not going to talk about Amy's murder."

Paige resisted a sigh as she resumed her seat on the small vinyl sofa while Seth perched on the edge of the coffee table across from her.

"I know this has been an upsetting day," he started, his elbows on his knees, hands clasped together. "This won't take long, then we'll get out of here."

There was something about the way Seth leaned in and the burdensome glint in his dark brown eyes that sent a prickly sensation racing along the nape of Paige's neck. Like he was about to drop some sort of new bombshell. Some other *incriminating* nonsense to heap on her brother's case.

Paige took a deep breath, hoping she was misreading him. Which could well be the case, given the anxiety clawing at her chest. And it didn't help that she'd hit brick walls at every juncture since she arrived back in Boone. Add in Amy's murder and the thought of one more emotional blow seemed overwhelming.

But she couldn't buckle. Couldn't let Seth see the emotional brokenness she was struggling with. She was tired, weary. But that information would only encourage him to push harder for her to leave. And there was more at stake than her. Trey needed to stay first priority.

Paige tried to prepare herself emotionally to keep fighting. Leaning against the arm of the sofa, she prayed her face wasn't giving anything away. "Okay, what questions do you have?"

Seth looked tired. Perplexed. Like the puzzle pieces weren't fitting. "Did Trey ever mention Madison having a stake in the family trust fund?"

For a moment Paige thought he was kidding. Trey

made a fairly good living as head of security for the local pulp mill, and Madison worked for the family business, and yet Paige recalled Trey often complaining that they struggled to make ends meet. Madison liked nice things, and Trey was generous to a fault, never wanting her to do without. Paige chalked up their struggles to those issues. But a *trust fund*? That didn't make sense.

"No. I never heard anything about a trust fund." She eyed Seth closely and shook her head. "Don't you remember the couple times we met Trey and Madison for dinner? We picked up the tab. They never had any money."

Tilting his head, Seth regarded her through narrowed eyes. "Well, apparently Madison did have money. Or access to it."

Another jaw-dropping statement. Paige firmed up her chin and sat up straighter. Had Trey known about a trust fund and hidden it from her? No sooner did that thought form in her head than an even more disturbing question appeared. Even if Trey had known, why would that information be relevant now? She looked at Seth blankly. "If Madison had a trust fund, obviously my brother didn't have access to it, so why bring it up now?"

For a moment Seth just sat there, and the quiet that followed ratcheted up Paige's heart rate and her concern. All of her effort to discover new evidence to help her brother's case and Seth stumbled on something new. And of course, he'd try to use it against Trey.

"Money is a strong motivator," Seth finally said. "So the trust fund is definitely something we'll look into and try to figure out if it played a part in Madison's murder."

Paige's heart dropped. "Do you really think Trey killed Madison over money?" She couldn't help the irritated look she shot at Seth. "You knew him better than that."

For a moment Seth said nothing, his face neutral, but

the doubting look in his eyes told her once again they didn't agree. "People can change when things get difficult."

She got that, all right. She thumped her arms over her chest. But now wasn't the time to broach their issues.

"Trey was losing his marriage and his wife," Seth went on. "We have to consider that the money in combination with everything else could have pushed him or anyone over the edge."

She disagreed, even if it sort of made sense—for someone other than her brother, that was. Trey was never driven by status or greed. *Like Gentry.*

As that thought slammed into her brain, Paige met Seth's gaze boldly. "Have you considered Gentry may have killed his sister for her share of the trust?" She blew a short burst of air through her lips. Of course he had; it seemed obvious.

"It's too early to make that assumption." Seth gave his pat answer, his expression revealing nothing. "But we'll explore every angle, every possible motive."

Of course he didn't want her to get her hopes up, but Paige couldn't help the little burst of optimism that flittered through her.

"But it is a viable possibility?" She just wanted to clarify.

Seth's stoic expression stayed intact. He straightened, shoulders back. "If the evidence supports it."

Renewed frustration zigzagged along Paige's nerve endings. *Evidence.* What about a gut feeling? For her, it made perfect sense. She didn't bother to bring that up. But there was one question she couldn't hold back. "How would a trust fund tie into Amy's murder?"

"Maybe Amy knew about the trust." Seth's voice was calm. "Or she may have had suspicions of what was going on with the attacks on you. Either way, she knew something the killer didn't want out. Given what we know so far, an act of revenge toward your brother is still our direction. And Amy got caught in the middle of it. Now we're charged with figuring out whether Gentry or someone else is responsible."

Guilt over Amy's death fed even more into her dampened spirit over the discovery of Madison's trust fund. One more thing to fuel speculation against her brother. She should have known Seth would see it that way. Which didn't deter her in the least. Her focus was still on her brother's freedom. With his court date in less than a week now, every minute counted. And sitting around the sheriff's office wasn't helping a thing.

She got to her feet. "Would you be able to take me home now?" She almost hated to ask, but Brett was busy working on the case, and she didn't want to pull him from that.

Seth eyed her a moment, his gaze burdened with concern that stole her breath and warmed her soul as readily as his touch. "The condo? Are you sure you feel comfortable being there alone?"

Yes. She nodded. More comfortable there than being here with Seth. At least there she could keep a handle on her erratic emotions.

"All right." He got to his feet.

She pulled her jacket tight, buttoning it, grateful he didn't press her. She was a big girl capable of taking care of herself—with God's help and direction.

Paige stayed close by Seth's side as he escorted her through the investigative bureau's wing of the sheriff's department. Long hallways, rooms on either side, large conference rooms, each with open doors. The place hadn't changed. Still a beehive of activity. Plainclothes detectives, clerks, secretaries all milling about. Phones ringing, keyboards tapping. Everyone busy, trying to solve the violent crime offenses in Watauga County.

They now had one more on their plate.

Paige swallowed back tears and stepped up her pace. She was so ready to get out of there. But as she breathed a sigh of relief, a wave of sadness swept in to wash it away. This morning, as she left the condo, she'd had big hopes for her day. A meeting with Amy. And hopefully some clues to get the ball rolling in her own investigation. None of which came to fruition. Instead, she was back at square one.

Even worse, Amy was now dead.

And the killer is getting more desperate, Paige thought with a shiver. He'd blatantly killed Amy. And she knew he wasn't going to stop there.

And she was no closer to proving her brother innocent than before she stepped foot back in Boone.

Lord, help to get me on the right track.

They came to the end of the hall, rounded the corner and stepped into the main lobby. Bright. Airy. Behind a nice new mahogany reception desk, the state and United States flags hung from wall-mounted poles. The entire west-facing wall was a series of floor-to-ceiling windows—the newest renovation to the historic building. One more thing that had changed since she'd been gone.

Swallowing a sigh, Paige directed her steps across the waxed cedar floor and through the double glass doors. A few steps outside, she pulled Seth to an abrupt stop. Just beyond the covered stoop, a pack of media hounds congregated along the granite steps, some gripping cameras and microphones, others scribbling on notepads.

Reporters.

Paige felt her shoulders droop, a sliver of dread curling

through her. Since she arrived, she'd stood her ground, tried to stay strong, kept it together, but the scene before her could likely do her in. With painful clarity, she recalled how in the early days after her brother's arrest journalists hounded her relentlessly. They'd camped outside her home. Followed her to work. Even called and left messages on her cell phone.

Squaring her shoulders, she pivoted toward Seth. "Why are they here?" She gestured with a nod toward the group and then added, "Not to talk to me, I ho—"

Before she even got the words out, the rash of media started toward her, cameras focused, microphones extended, questions coming in quick succession.

"Is it true you just witnessed the scene of a murder?"

"Do you think Amy's murder was in any way tied to your sister-in-law's death?"

"How did you know the victim?"

"Why were you at the victim's home?"

Astonished and unnerved, Paige stood motionless, her thoughts still blurred in the agony of Amy's death. She wasn't ready for this.

"Come on, let's get out of here." Seth took her arm and steered her rapidly back into the building and down the hallway. Seth kept one guiding hand on her back. Her heart pounded in her chest. Which, she told herself, had nothing to do with Seth, only the adrenaline thundering in her veins from the press being there.

"We'll go out through the back. The parking lot isn't far from there."

She nodded absently, her stomach churning, her legs heavy. They stopped at the secondary elevator and she finally got up the nerve to ask, "Am I a suspect?"

"No, you're not a suspect," Seth said calmly, but the way his jaw tightened left no room for confusion as to his feelings about the situation brewing outside. "But the sister of Madison's suspected killer stumbling on the scene of another murder obviously piqued their interest."

She gritted her teeth. Undeniably, great story material. A second brutal murder in Boone and another Becker found at the scene.

Another chill settled deep in Paige's bones. Trey had been first on the scene of Madison's murder, and he was now standing trial for her death.

The elevator doors opened. They stepped inside, took it down one floor to the basement and continued down the long hall that led them outside into the cool October air. Seth stepped out first into an alley that ran between the sheriff's department and the courthouse and jail. Before she could follow, he shot up his hand. "Hold on."

She waited in the doorway as Seth gave a thorough sweep of the area.

"Okay, let's go."

Five minutes later they were safe in the confines of his truck. As Seth revved the engine to life, she clipped the seat belt into place, a slight victory swelling in her chest until the sudden *tap-tap-tap* on the passenger window caused a surge of panic.

Whipping around to stare out through the glass, Paige came face-to-face with a shorter, slightly built man with a graying head of mussed-up hair and dark beady eyes. He held up the press badge around his neck. "Reporter, ma'am."

No kidding. She swung back around and locked gazes with Seth, but not before she got a glimpse of the name on the badge. *Clark Rogers.* He was one of the journalists who'd covered Madison's murder. Former Navy SEAL Brutally Murders Estranged Wife. His biased interpretation of the so-called evidence made headlines and went viral, sensationalizing her brother's arrest.

The last thing she wanted was more bad press for her brother or for Rogers to somehow make more out of her being at the murder scene. Even for a witness, she knew information could be misconstrued, as with the case of her brother.

Seth must have sensed her discomfort, for he jammed the gearshift into Reverse before he cocked an eyebrow at her.

"Can you please take me home now?" she asked.

"The condo's gated, but the media probably figured out a way to get in."

Her panic bumped up a notch, escalating further when she heard another tap on the glass. "Miss Becker, I just have a few questions?" Rogers's voice filtered through the closed window.

No, thank you. Paige didn't bother giving him the courtesy of that response. She blinked up at Seth. "Then would you mind taking me somewhere out of the watchful eye of reporters?"

"I know just the place." Seth stepped on the gas. They barreled out the parking lot and headed south, leaving Rogers and his comrades in their dust.

Five miles from the edge of town, Seth directed the vehicle down Highway 321, then turned right down an unmarked country road. It was a pocked and rutted half-mile stretch of dirt and gravel surrounded by heavy forest that encircled the stocked pond on the eastern border of his property.

The truck wheels, digging into the soft earth, spewed up rock and dust as he swerved to avoid downed limbs, small uprooted trees and other debris. The private drive leading to his cabin was in worse condition than usual, still bearing the effects of the recent storm.

Slowing down, Seth turned left. The rustic log house appeared around the slight bend in the road at the top of a rise. "Almost there." He looked over at Paige.

She nodded, looking a little somber. Probably still mulling over the events of the day. Or had coming back to this spot stirred up old memories of better times? Maybe he was delusionary to think she missed this place. Part of him even liked to think she missed him, too.

Seth struck that last thought. Hardly relevant to what the future held. They'd both moved on to new ventures in their lives and there was no going back, he reiterated to himself firmly.

Seth parked in his usual spot just outside the garage. He grabbed his laptop and climbed out, but before he could get around to the passenger side, Paige was already out on the driveway, taking in the view.

Nestled in stands of lush evergreens and soaring hardwoods, the house hadn't changed much in the ten months since she'd left town. Seth never seemed to have enough time to work on it. Or, more accurately, motivation to finish the work.

Judging from the way Paige's gaze kept straying across the front porch, stacked high with boxes and still missing pieces of front railing, she was having those same thoughts. She'd been instrumental in a lot of the design and construction of the place. And had spent a lot of time visiting and working alongside him.

As they approached the front door, Seth could already hear Laser scratching to come out. Immediately after he opened the door, the dog burst through it, barking and with his tail wagging as he ran circles around Paige's feet.

It had been a long time since Seth had seen his dog

react with enthusiasm like that. Twelve years old and going blind, but he obviously didn't have a problem recognizing Paige. "Thanks, buddy. I barely get a tail wag when I get home. And that's only if I'm hefting a bag of dog chow over my shoulder."

Paige chuckled. "I'm sure that's not true." She immediately crouched down beside Laser, running her fingers through his thick coat. "How are you, boy?"

Laser nuzzled up against her. The happy dance stopped, but he was now serenading them with a high-pitched whimper, earning him an extra hug from Paige.

Seth couldn't help but laugh. The old mutt knew how to play it up. Despite everything, Seth felt a rush of warmth at just having Paige back in his house. A temporary moment of insanity that he let linger a moment before he shook it off and regained his senses.

Okay. Enough of that. Seth stepped into the house and shrugged out of his jacket, hanging it on a hook on the wall. "Dinner, anyone?"

Laser broke out of Paige's grasp with a hardy bark. He took off for the kitchen, paws skittering and scratching against the hardwood floor.

"I'll take that as a yes." He flashed a quick smile at Paige. "How about you? Are you hungry?"

A slight shrug and she smiled. "Yeah. Actually, I could eat something."

In the kitchen as Seth hunkered down to feed Laser, he put Paige to work foraging through the pantry and fridge. He thought it might be best to leave the meal planning to her. His creativity in the kitchen stopped at canned sardines on crackers or peanut butter and jelly sandwiches. And he wasn't even sure he had what it took to make those.

"Sorry, Paige, I should have stopped on our way here

and picked something up." Although his focus had been to get her out of the limelight and to safe shelter. Then again, if he had stopped, it would have given her an opportunity to change her mind about coming here. Even now, he was half wondering how long she'd stick around.

Paige poked her head out of the refrigerator. "That's fine. There's plenty here. How about a ham and American cheese quesadilla with green chiles and avocado?"

Nope. He never would have thought of that.

"Oh. And green olives on the side."

Why not? "Sounds good. Let's do it."

Thirty minutes later, he took a seat across from her at the table. Paige offered a blessing, and for once, he didn't find himself fidgeting in his seat, waiting for her to finish up. In fact, once she was through, he even offered a firm amen.

Paige responded with a surprised smile, and he couldn't help but smile himself.

He reveled in the small victory of seeing her pleased as they dug into their food. She'd always told him he was missing out not having God in his life. He was beginning to understand.

The impromptu meal Paige had prepared was good. She had always been a good cook, but she didn't usually have to pull a meal together with a handful of miscellaneous ingredients. Seth was impressed. "Paige, it all tastes great. Thanks." He finally set down his fork by his plate.

"You're welcome." She got up from her chair and took her plate to the sink.

The silence that came next served only to remind him of why he brought Paige here in the first place. He wanted her safe. Not just for today, but for the rest of her time in Boone. As much as he hated to broach the subject, especially now, when they were actually enjoying a peaceful, civil moment between them, he knew it needed to be done.

He pushed up from the chair and wandered over to where Paige stood at the sink. "Let's talk about your plans."

"What do you mean by plans?" She turned around, drying her hands on a dish towel.

"You know, what's on your agenda as far as your plans to help your brother," he said, trying for a casual conversation.

But immediately, Paige eyed him with open suspicion. She crossed her arms over her chest, leaving the towel dangling from her fingers. "Please, Seth, don't press me on this. I'm not leaving town."

The tension in the room amped up, and he could just about feel the stress radiating from her.

"Whoa. Time out." Seth crisscrossed his hands above his head. "I'm not asking you to leave."

"You're not?" Paige's frown smoothed out, and she softened her tone. "Good. Because I'm tired of that argument."

So was he. "I'm not saying I agree with your decision to stick around," he clarified, not wanting to be misunderstood. "However, as long as you're here, I'd like for you to be someplace safe. So—"

"Oh, no…" Paige straightened, cutting him off. "You're not planning to keep me holed up here to keep me out of the investigation?"

Though her tone was almost joking, the near-panicked look in her eyes ripped a hole in his heart.

Did she actually think he would ever hold her against her will? If so, he hoped the assumption was stress induced, because regardless of their differences, she should trust him more than that.

Seth planted his hands on his hips. "If you're asking if I planned to kidnap you, the answer is no."

"Kidnapping?" Paige winced, color heightening in her cheeks. "Sorry, Seth. I never meant to imply that. I guess my brain just isn't thinking clearly."

The pain he saw in her eyes stirred him. It was all he could do to stay where he was and not pull her into his arms to comfort her. But that would only add more stress to the situation.

He hauled in a deep breath. "I understand." He grinned and said, "That's why it would be better if you stay here. We can work together, and you'll be in a safe place."

"Work together?" Paige's skeptical expression creased the corners of her green eyes.

"Chief Mullins pulled me back on your case." Seth's muscles tensed as he waited for her to object. She didn't. Instead, her lips parted as if she had something to say, then she stopped, lips tight again.

"With the investigation into Amy's murder just beginning, we need to consider how it's tied to Madison's murder. So I'll work with Brett. I'll be happy to listen to any information you have, and we'll see what we come up with."

"So," Paige said after a moment, "are you saying you believe my brother might not be guilty?"

Seth wouldn't go that far. "Let's see what evidence we come up with first."

She leaned back against the counter, nibbling on her lower lip, before she nodded. "Okay. Deal."

"Okay, but the one caveat to all this is that I want you to stay here. So you'll be safe," he reiterated. And so he could get a decent night's sleep.

She pushed away from the counter, shaking her head. "I can't just stay here. I can go to a motel or stay with a friend."

"And put more people at risk?" Seth raised an eyebrow, not willing to lose this battle. "Someone's been on your tail since you arrived. Being out there on your own milling around town will only afford him more opportunity to get to you."

Paige's lips pursed in disgust as she crossed her arms over her chest. "Thanks for the reminder. Still, I wouldn't feel right being alone here with you."

Nothing like being blunt. It was obvious trust was still a long way off. His heart kicked at that. Seth shifted his weight. "I understand and wouldn't expect you to do that. So I arranged for someone else to stay here with us." More eyes, more ears always a plus.

"You asked someone to come here to stay with us?" Paige echoed, raising an eyebrow at him. "And who would that someone be?"

Seth hesitated a moment, and then he smiled. "My mother."

Paige borrowed an old shirt and extra toothbrush from Seth and then set off up the stairs to get ready for bed. After the long day she'd had, she was exhausted and ready for sleep. She'd just spent two hours looking up numbers and contacting three of Madison's other coworkers, hoping to get some insight on what Amy might have known or suspected. But instead of garnering information, she'd been belittled, yelled at and hung up on. One person even threatened to call the police if she tried to contact them again.

So, like the rest of her day, unproductive. No one

would talk to her, let alone discuss Madison's murder. They already had her brother tried and convicted.

And the one possible advocate Trey had, Amy, was now dead. Fighting back tears, Paige stepped into the guest room. With a deep breath, she resolved to shelve all thoughts of her brother's case for tonight.

She was grateful Seth didn't seem to mind that she wouldn't be up when his mother arrived. Not that she disliked Ruby Garrison. On the contrary, Ruby was more of a mother than she'd ever had.

But her breakup with Seth had left a lot of loose ends, and Ruby was one of them. Through no fault of Ruby's, Paige hadn't spoken to her since the relationship ended. She just couldn't force herself to answer Ruby's calls. She was dealing with enough with her brother's arrest, and trying to rationalize feelings about Seth didn't exactly feel like a top priority.

Distraught, grief-stricken, frustrated, broken. That pretty much summed up Paige by the time she left Boone. Then as more time wore on, she could think of fewer and fewer reasons to contact Ruby.

Paige pulled back the quilt and adjusted the pillows on the bed, feeling a slight twinge of guilt for not staying up. With a deep sigh, she climbed under the sheets. In truth, the last thing she needed today was to get tied up in one more awkward situation.

Paige tugged up the quilt and closed her eyes, trying to clear the cobwebs in her brain and focus on sleep.

Vaguely, she registered the sound of scratching when the door creaked open and Laser bounded in.

"No, boy—" She started to stop him, but before she even sat up, Laser lunged onto the bed and started making himself comfortable on the corner of the mattress.

She scooted over a little to give him more room. "Good night, puppy." Paige laughed through a yawn.

Another battle not worth fighting, and strange to say, she really didn't mind. It had been a long time since she'd felt this loved or missed. Ten months, to be exact. She snuggled beneath the covers, feeling safer just having Laser around. And if she was honest, Seth being downstairs gave her even more peace of mind. A temporary fix that she savored for the moment.

SEVEN

"Okay, pack what you need and let's get in and out quickly," Seth said, his eyes riveted to the windshield, alert and watchful as they pulled into the condo's parking lot.

"Got it." Paige kept low in the truck's cab, out of sight of any reporters that might be lurking about. He hoped that with news of Amy's murder still making headlines, Paige's attacker would also lie low for a while.

Seth parked and climbed out of the truck. He took a quick survey of the area while Paige waited inside. Everything looked clear. He peeked back through the window, giving her a thumbs-up. "All right. Let's go."

They headed up the stairs to the third floor. He stayed close to Paige, intent on keeping her safe and making this a quick trip.

Once inside the condo, Seth positioned himself in the entry, the best possible place to keep an eye on both Paige and any activity outside the front door.

This wasn't an ideal scenario, having to contend with Paige as he tried to narrow down who her attacker was. But for the time being, at least, Paige was by his side instead of trying to track down leads to solve Trey's case and getting herself into more trouble.

Seth looked at his watch—6:40 a.m.—as Paige bustled about the small condo, gathering personal items and packing her bags. He wanted to get out of there before morning traffic was in full gear. They had a full day of brainstorming ahead of them. "Ready?"

"I think I've got everything." She slung her computer bag over her shoulder, and Seth grabbed her rolling suitcase.

"Do you really think my attacker would dare to come around here?" Paige asked as they started back down the stairs. "I mean, with all the press running around town, he'd be crazy to try anything now."

She was looking for reassurance, and Seth didn't blame her. He only wished things in life were that clearcut. Logic only went so far when it came to murder. Even being in a gated community wasn't much of a deterrent for someone with an agenda to kill.

"So, what do you think?" She nudged his elbow. "Maybe he's scared and has gone into hiding?"

Her wishful thinking struck at his heart, and Seth responded with a quick glance and a wink. "Let's not hang around and find out," he said, playing it cool. He didn't want to alarm her, even as every nerve ending stayed on high alert. People with an agenda stopped at nothing. And this guy was brazen; he didn't scare easy. But if Paige's attacker's goal was to get to her, he'd better be prepared to contend with Seth first.

They stepped onto the ground floor from the stairs, and as they kept walking, Seth surveyed around them. No sign of anyone, at least that he could see. He strained his ears to listen.

Nothing. The place was empty. Silent.

Paige started talking, offering a long-winded update

on her brother. Her favorite subject, and a difficult topic he planned to pick her brain about later.

As they continued along the sidewalk, he slowed his pace. A subtle noise caught his attention. A rustling of leaves, maybe. Then a branch snapped.

With his hand hovering over his gun, Seth wheeled around toward the sound. He panned his gaze down the walkway and into the bordering tree line. Nothing came into view.

"What is it?" Seth could read the fear in her eyes as she gazed up at him.

"Hopefully nothing. But time to get going." He cupped her left elbow and steered her toward the parking lot. The feeling of dread settled into a hard knot in his gut.

Instinct told him something was off. And he'd learned a long time ago not to ignore his gut, because it was usually right.

They came to the end of the walkway, and as they stepped off the curb and onto the asphalt, three rapid gunshots ripped through the air, echoing like crackling thunder.

"No!" Paige screamed. Her shoulder bag hit the ground as she dropped for cover, crouching beside it, throwing her arms over her head.

Seth spun toward her, Glock raised. "Come on, let's get out of here." He grabbed Paige's hand, pulling her to run. They took off in a sprint, skirting around vehicles, his gaze swinging back and forth across the lot, trying to get a handle on where to go next.

More gunshots came from behind. Bullets whizzed past their heads.

"This way," Seth yelled and ducked right, pulling Paige with him. They rounded the corner into a smaller lot in the back of the complex just as another burst of gunshots lit the air like fireworks. Glass shattered, spitting jagged shards into the air in all directions.

"Seth! We're going to get killed!" Paige's panicked scream echoed above the explosive din.

Not if he could help it. Jacked on adrenaline, Seth took stock of the area and then gestured with his gun toward a packed row of parked cars. "Paige, get down. Over there."

Jerking from his grip, Paige darted right and flew for cover, ducking between two cars as Seth took off to the left. He hopped a low fence and then made his way up a small hill as fast as his boots could navigate the rain-soaked terrain, trying to get back to the front of Tessa's condo unit.

More gunfire erupted. He looked back, teeth gritted at the sound of shattering glass. A cold knot of fear coiled in his gut. What if Paige had been hit? He slashed that last thought. Feelings and emotions had no place on the job. And right now his job was to take down a killer.

He picked up speed, and using the retaining block wall as a shield, he worked his way back to where the shots had been fired.

At the end of the brick embankment, he skidded to a stop, finding himself right back where he started. Breathing hard, he perked his ears and listened. A shuffling noise came from his left. He whipped his gaze around, searching for a person, a shadow. And he spotted something, a movement in the row of bushes across from him.

Seth slipped from his hiding spot and inched his way along the tree-dotted walk, keeping alert for any more gunfire. When he reached a thick wooden post that served as a marker for the walking trails in the community, he leaned up against it. He leveled his gun and projected his voice. "This is the Watauga County Sheriff's Department. Drop your weapon and step out with your hands up."

The silence that came next was unsettling. Deafening.

Seth yanked out his cell phone, speed-dialed for backup. *God, if You're watching out there, please take care of Paige.*

Gun ready, heart racing, Seth waited. Time ticked by. His adrenaline, already through the roof, sparked higher at the sudden roar of an approaching automobile. He jerked a look over his shoulder to see a small SUV turn into the parking lot.

It was traveling slowly. Seth eased around the wood post to the other side. From that vantage point he could see there were two people inside. They were talking. Probably oblivious to danger lurking just outside their doors.

The SUV pulled to a stop. Seth held his breath as they parked in an open spot. Away from other parked vehicles. Right out in the open. Without even realizing it, they were stepping into a war zone.

No. Seth cringed as he saw them start to unbuckle. Still talking. Still oblivious. *Just stay in the car.* He tightened his grip on his Glock, mentally chanting the order.

Come on. Come on, guys. Where are you? Seth craned his neck, hoping to see flashing lights. He needed his comrades here now.

His gaze landed back on the couple's car. He watched as the door opened. The man stepped out. A deep yawn as he did a quick stretch, waiting near the hood of the vehicle as the woman climbed out of the passenger door.

Silence. Deadly silence. Seth swung his gaze down the highway. No signs of law enforcement or the shooter. Maybe the creep had taken off.

A shot cracked, and an earsplitting scream followed.

Seth looked past the man to see Paige in the main parking area. She was in a frantic run, zigzagging around vehicles, leaping over concrete parking bumpers. Before Seth could do anything, panicked gasps and squeals flew from the man and woman as they ran to Paige's aid.

No! Busting away from his hiding spot, Seth hollered down through the lot, making himself a target, as well. "Shooter! Get down!"

An instant later, another shot rang out, and the man crumpled to the asphalt, blood gushing from his lower limb. *Oh, no!* Paige's voice crashed into his ears as she dropped down beside him.

"Get him between the vehicles."

As Paige and the woman pulled the man to safety, another shot whooshed past his head. Anger burned like an inferno in his chest. He was ready to take this guy down. He spun and dropped to a squatting position beside a small sedan. He lifted his weapon. Aimed. He was ready.

He wildly whipped his gaze around, watching for movement. A shadow. Anything. *Come on, coward. Show yourself.* Minutes passed. His heart pounded.

Then from the east side of the lot, Seth heard the loud roar of an engine. He jerked his gaze over his shoulder to see a truck in a smaller dirt-and-gravel construction lot peel out, kicking up dust in its wake.

White truck. Long bed. Extended cab. Fury kicked Seth's pulse into overdrive. *Paige's perpetrator.* The driver gunned it out of the lot and down a service road.

No way! Seth huffed out a breath through clenched teeth and lowered his gun. He tucked it into his waistband holster beneath his leather jacket and pulled out his phone. He called dispatch with a description. But in his heart of hearts, he knew there was no stopping this guy.

At least not today.

God, I think I'm going to need Your help on this one.
For a second time that day, an automatic prayer came.
Seth couldn't explain it and actually felt at peace at the
relationship he was gaining.

Paige pushed up from her crouch and took a step back
as EMS medics took over. The man, pale and shivering,
was hefted onto a stretcher, his distressed moans echoing around them.

His wife stood off to the side, hands over her face,
shaking and sobbing. Paige had learned that the couple
were newlyweds, just home from their honeymoon. She
rubbed the woman's shoulder as medics strapped her
husband on the gurney. "It's going to be okay. Please
hang in there."

The woman nodded, even as she sobbed harder.

Her husband had taken a bullet to the left leg,
midthigh. With Seth's help Paige had been able to slow
the bleeding by wrapping the man's leg with a blanket
from the couple's vehicle. He'd been alert. Oriented. Even
managed to answer a few questions. He looked like was
going to make it. One blessing amid the chaos.

"Paige, are you ready?" Seth's deep voice soothed over
her frazzled nerves as he came up beside her. He was
her hero today. "Brett's going to hang out on the scene
for a while."

More than ready. She nodded. "I hope you guys catch
that creep."

"Me, too," Seth agreed, wrapping a comforting arm
around her shoulder. "Let's get out of here."

Paige leaned into his protective hold, knowing it was a
dangerous place to be, but she felt helpless to pull away,
especially as she thought about how close her attacker had

gotten once again. And he wasn't going to rest until he accomplished his plan. Her stomach cramped at that reality.

On unsteady legs she walked with Seth into the parking lot. A chill needled her deep to the bone as her gaze took in the collateral damage left from targeted attacks on her life—rows of parked vehicles, pocked and riddled with bullets, shattered glass and shiny shell casings. Evidence and more evidence, and still no suspect to be apprehended.

Would she ever feel safe again?

She breathed deep to settle her prickly nerves. Hopefully, they could learn something about her attacker from all this.

Back at the cabin, as Seth walked straight to his office to do some research on his computer, Paige melted against the entry wall and pulled in a deep breath. Seth was tough, she'd have to give him that. He'd just spent the morning dodging bullets, and his nerves appeared perfectly intact. While she, on the other hand, could barely breathe. And she wasn't sure how much more she could take.

Fighting the fleeting impulse to just pack up and head home to Durham, Paige fixated on a faint glow of hope that with Seth's help she could finally uncover the truth. Only six days until her brother's trial, but she now had Seth on her team. *Sort of*, she reminded herself.

A high-pitched whistle sounded, and Paige jumped up and straightened as her mind flooded with the horrific events of yesterday's murder. Fighting back tears, she shoved the memories aside and refocused. Her emotions were tattered enough without reliving that nightmare.

Quickly, she shrugged out of her coat, hanging it on a hook by the door. She was a guest in Seth's house, and as awkward as it was, she still needed to be sociable.

As she crossed the threshold into the kitchen, she found Ruby pulling the squealing kettle from the stove. A savory scent lingered in the air, reminding her she hadn't eaten breakfast yet. Actually, she decided, after the morning she'd had and the churning in her stomach, she was better off.

Ruby lingered, her back to Paige as she filled her cup.

Paige sucked in a deep breath, still not a hundred percent comfortable with her accommodations, or the people she was sharing them with.

"Good morning." Paige strove for jovial, although *frazzled* was more accurate.

Ruby turned around, steeping a tea bag in her steamy cup. "Oh, Paige. Good morning." She broke into a smile.

She seemed genuinely happy to see her, making Paige feel guilty for her tentative nerves and not waiting up last night to see her.

"You and Seth were up and out the door early," Ruby continued. "I was beginning to wonder when you'd be back."

Paige actually had those same thoughts. "I had some things at the condo I needed to get. But we're back now." She offered a small smile and didn't elaborate, deciding it was better to spare Ruby the disturbing details of the morning shoot-out for the time being. She remembered how she worried about Seth.

"Good. I hope you got what you needed. Now, how about some breakfast? I have bacon already cooked, and I could whip you up a couple eggs?"

"Oh, no, thank you." Paige's acid-soaked stomach wasn't quite ready for food. "But I might have some tea." She pointed to the cabinet over the microwave. "Does Seth still keep the coffee and tea there?"

"He sure does." Ruby nodded tightly, the overhead

lights picking up the silver highlighting her short bob of mahogany hair. "I don't think he's changed much of anything since you two split up." Her tone was melancholy. And no one better than Ruby to bear testimony to the disheartening effects of their breakup. She was never one to keep her opinions to herself—like her son.

"Some people are slow to change things." Paige forced a laugh, trying to keep things light, even though the reference to their previous relationship sent a sick roll through her midsection. Not the conversation she wanted to get into right now. Talking about a failed relationship with her ex-boyfriend's mother didn't feel right. Especially with her conflicting emotions from just being around Seth again battling inside.

"Awesome. Peppermint." Paige changed the subject, plucking the tea bag out of the box. One of her favorite stress remedies. "So, Ruby, I hear you've been doing some remodeling," she said and went to grab a mug.

Leaning a hip against the counter, Ruby gave a deep sigh. "Oh, my, yes. Lots of updates. New cabinets, carpet, paint. Seth's been a great help. Next I'll be looking for new furniture."

"Sounds like a fun project," Paige said, filling her cup, trying to ignore the little twist in her gut when she thought about the plans she and Seth had had for this house. Warm colors. Rustic decor. Timber spindles on the sprawling front porch where one day they'd planned to be married.

Biting her lip to hold in a sigh, she dropped her tea bag in her cup and killed those thoughts. Dreams, as it turned out.

"The project has been keeping me busy, to say the least." Ruby carried her cup and saucer over to the table and took a seat. "So, Paige, what have you been up to these last few months?"

Paige nearly choked on the sip she'd taken. Nothing as fun as remodeling, that was for sure. She swallowed tightly and cleared her throat, not wanting to get into her brother's drama. "I've been working as a substance abuse counselor for a rehab clinic in Durham. That's been keeping me pretty busy."

"I imagine it would." Ruby tilted her head ever so slightly, a look of understanding in her eyes. "So, how's your brother doing?"

Paige's heart thudded, as it always did when the topic of her brother came up. "My brother? He's doing okay." As well as could be expected, given the circumstances. Paige joined Ruby at the table, part of her not even wanting to get into this conversation. "He has a court date coming up. I'm sure Seth told you that I'm back in town trying to see what I can come up with to help his case."

"Yes, he mentioned that you've had some trouble trying to do that." She shook her head. "It can be a dangerous world out there."

Yes, it can. Paige agreed with a short nod and then returned to her tea.

"Well, I'm glad you're okay, and I hope you find the information you need to help him." Raising her teacup, Ruby gently blew on the vapors.

Paige slowly turned in her chair to eye her more closely. She was skeptical. Ruby was so nonchalant. She'd barely batted an eye at Paige trying to help Trey. Paige lifted the mug to her lips and took a long sip. Maybe people weren't as judgmental as she once thought.

Sweet relief mingled with a stab of guilt. Maybe she was the one that was being judgmental. Harboring resentment for what she perceived others were thinking.

An interesting thought she'd never considered and one she'd have to process awhile.

"But Paige," Ruby said, after a moment, "whatever the outcome is for your brother, you'll have to accept it and pick up and get on with your life."

She must have been talking to Seth. Paige had heard that same argument since her brother's arrest. *Paige, you can't let yourself get sucked into Trey's issues. Be there for him. Be supportive, but don't let his mistakes ruin your life.* Seth's words rattled in her head. As daunting today as the day she'd first heard them. He could never get her passion or unwavering belief in her brother's innocence. And in truth, he still didn't.

But now, here she sat, sipping tea and listening to Seth's mother give her the same advice. Resting against the wooden rungs of the chair, Paige took another long drink, trying to slow her heartbeat, trying to keep her cool. Ruby was concerned, Paige knew that. But it still stung her heart to consider moving on with her life while her brother was stuck behind bars for a crime he didn't commit.

She took a deep breath. "Thanks, Ruby, I appreciate your concern." Intense emotions flooded her, upping her anxiety as reality crashed back in. Six days until her brother's trial. If they didn't come up with something, he would likely be spending the rest of his life behind bars. Suddenly nauseated, she set her cup down with a clink.

And right now they had nothing substantial.

Paige felt a warm hand on her shoulder, and she flinched. She glanced back and lifted her eyebrows at Seth.

"Sorry, I didn't mean to startle you." He stared down at her, a sheepish look on his face.

"No worries." She waved it off as she willed her erratic pulse to slow. More annoyed by the way she reacted to Seth's touch. Something that needed to stop, she chastised herself. "So, how did your research go?"

"Actually, good." As Ruby slipped out of the room, Seth settled into the seat beside her, a grin in his eyes.

"Before you say anything else, I want to thank you for today. You saved my life. Actually, for the second time." She smiled, brushing a wisp of hair from her face.

"A second time?" His brows rose.

"Two days ago you saved me from being pounded by a piece of siding."

"Oh, yeah." His mouth twisted in a teasing grin that sent butterflies erupting in her stomach. "That would have hurt."

To say the least. She rolled her eyes with a chuckle. "And getting hit by bullets doesn't sound like much fun, either."

"No problem. Just part of the job."

The job? Her heart took a nosedive. "Well, good job, then," she said, almost cringing and mentally kicking herself for venturing to think Seth had a more personal agenda when it came to her. When would she learn to leave the past alone? Get a grip and move on.

Seth sat up straighter, his eyes widening as if he could read her mind. Her disenchantment was probably written all over her face. "Of course I'm worried about you, and I'll do whatever it takes to keep you safe."

Good try. But he didn't owe her an explanation. She stiffened and lifted her chin. "I appreciate that. So, tell me what you dug up."

"Well." Seth shifted in his seat, looking as happy as she was to move on to a more productive topic. "This morning I asked Ted to look into the Cramers' trust account. And he came up with some interesting facts."

Hope ballooned in Paige's chest as she whirled in her seat to fully face Seth. Maybe this was the break they were looking for.

"Ted found that a month after Trey and Madison married, Madison changed the beneficiary on her portion of the trust from Gentry to Trey."

Paige's heart stopped. Had Trey known about that? If he had…

Her brain raced, and as doubt crowded in, for the first time ever she wondered if maybe she could be wrong and her brother was guilty.

A split second later the small voice inside her said, *Are you kidding?* She shook off the doubt. Trey was innocent. And there was no way he'd known about Madison's money. He never would have kept that from her. "So Madison never changed the beneficiary back after they separated?"

Seth shook his head. "Not that we can tell. According to the executor of Frank Cramer's will, who Ted spoke to, Madison contacted him several times after the separation, but only to request funds. Which is interesting, because Gentry led us to believe he usually petitioned for funds on her behalf."

"So…" Paige said, thinking out loud. "Either Gentry is lying or she went behind his back."

"Exactly."

Paige's eyes cut to his. "How much was Madison's share of the trust?"

"Three point five million."

A hefty amount. Paige's heart dropped, feeling confused. "How does all this tie into Madison's murder?" She was almost afraid to ask.

Seth shrugged. "Good question. I think it's time for another little talk with Gentry."

* * *

An hour later, Seth's GPS pointed him toward Boone's historic downtown. From King Street, he stayed left at the fork and kept traveling north for several miles. He'd just gotten off the phone with Brett, updating him on his plan to talk to Gentry. Although it was a bit of an afterthought. Seth was used to working alone. Had been since he joined the sheriff's department three years ago, and trying to keep someone up to speed on his every move was an expectation he needed to stay mindful of—though it required more effort than he'd expect even from a rookie detective.

But a promise was a promise, and he was willing to do whatever was necessary to keep peace with Brett and stay on his good side and on Paige's case. And from what he was sensing, the investigation on Madison's murder was also ready to crack wide-open. Clues were coming in. Now, if he could just fit the pieces together—and quickly, before Trey's court date next week.

At the stoplight, Seth checked his email and was disappointed that he still hadn't received a ballistics report from forensics on the bullets used in the morning shooting. He knew it was a long shot, even if they narrowed down the weapon type, to be able to find a possible link between the brand and model of the gun used and gun owners in the area. But he had to cover all bases, probably starting with the local rifle clubs and shooting ranges.

Seth pressed redial, trying forensics again. Frustrated, he left another message for them to update him as soon they made a positive determination. They were a diligent bunch, and he hated to push. But with a shooter loose on the street, every minute counted.

Seth turned into the Willoughby Hills neighborhood and began winding down the tree-lined drive that led to

Carol Ann Cramer's residence. Gentry and Madison's mother. Tall pines and patches of dense forest bordered the old Victorian house. To the right, heavy oak foliage formed a canopy over the road, and parked beneath it was a midsize black truck and a blue sports sedan bearing the distinctive CA & GM logo for Cramer's Antique and Gift Mart.

The sedan, he knew, was Gentry's.

Good. Seth hadn't wasted a trip. His first stop had been to the antique shop, where he spoke to Sarah, one of the employees. Like other employees who worked for Gentry, she was also hesitant to talk to him at first, but after a little pushing she finally told him where Gentry might be.

And her intuition paid off.

Seth parked at the end of the driveway and got out. After a careful sweep of the area, he started up the cobblestone walk. Nothing appeared amiss, but he did notice tufts of grass and weeds in the brick-lined flower beds in the yard and a cluster of dried-up, dead potted plants along the entry steps. A telltale sign that Mrs. Cramer wasn't around.

Otherwise, the place looked about the same as he remembered from the last time he'd been there, when he and Paige attended a dinner in honor of Trey and Madison when they were first married. A little family gathering after the impromptu wedding. And as Seth thought back, he also recalled a rather strained atmosphere throughout the evening. At the time it reminded him of the awkwardness of the two families not knowing each other. But it was more than that. The Cramers, who were sociable around town, he found were also private people. Quiet. Discreet. At least when it came to opening their home.

Seth stepped up to ring the doorbell, and before it even

sounded, the door swung open and a man Seth didn't recognize stood there. He was a thirtysomething, 250-pound
linebacker type, with cropped blond hair and a cold,
pointed stare.

"How can I help you?" The man crossed his thick
arms.

Seth flashed his badge. "Seth Garrison, detective for
the Watauga County Sheriff's Department. I'd like to
talk to Gentry Cramer."

"I'm sorry, that's not possible." The man's answer was
swift, with no regard for the fact that a law enforcement
officer was asking. "Mr. Cramer is on an international
call at the moment. I'm his assistant, Eli. What can I do
for you?"

The man watched Seth expectantly, like he was waiting for Seth to just hand him a business card and apologize for dropping by unannounced. "Actually, Eli, I'd
appreciate it if you'd tell Mr. Cramer that I'm here to
see him."

Eli's jaw tightened, and his shoulders went back.
Stance wide. Hands now balled on his hips. He meant to
intimidate. "Like I said, Mr. Garrison, that's not possible.
But I'll let him know that you stopped by."

Seth held Eli's stare for a long moment, hoping the
other man would catch his drift that his intimidation theory wasn't working. At six foot two and 220 pounds, Seth
wasn't easily bullied. But he was curious as to what Gentry was involved in that he'd need a bulldozer bodyguard
like Eli around. "Sorry, Eli, but I need to speak to Gentry. *Now.*" Seth put a heavy emphasis on that last word.

Eli's expression darkened like an approaching storm.
He opened his mouth, looking intent on shooting down
Seth's request, but then stopped and took a deep breath.
"I'll let Mr. Cramer know that you're here to see him."

"Thank you." Seth nodded.

Eli turned and disappeared down the hallway.

Finally. Seth braced his hand against the door frame, irritation building in his chest. *Games.* He had no patience for any more today.

Two minutes later Gentry came to the door, wearing the same miserable grimace as his guard dog, Eli, who stood rigidly beside him. "What is it now, Garrison? Has Paige gotten herself into more trouble?"

"Funny you should ask." Seth peered at him closely, trying to read him. "Actually, Paige was involved in a little fiasco this morning. To be more specific, she had shots fired at her in a parking lot."

With a shrug, Gentry met Seth's gaze without flinching. "Sounds like the girl needs to find better areas in town to hang out." He had an inscrutable expression etched on his face that gave nothing away.

"This took place at the Beaver Creek condo complex," Seth quipped with irritation. "A rather nice area of town."

"I just heard about that," Eli interjected, stepping in closer to the door. His expression sobered; his tough-guy facade cracked. "Is it true that the shooter is still on the loose?" The uneasiness in his tone mirrored how Seth felt about the situation.

"I'm afraid so."

"Things around Boone are getting crazy." Eli looked to Gentry with weary skepticism. "It seems that Madison's murder was just the tip of the iceberg. Now Amy's dead and someone's out there shooting up parking lots. And with Trey in jail there must be another crazy involved in all this."

"A crazy loose on the streets," Gentry corrected Eli curtly, shooting Seth a dark look. "And while the cops are breathing down my neck, that person's out there getting away with murder."

"That's the million-dollar question, isn't it, Gentry?" Seth replied, emulating Gentry's annoyed tone. "Who is that person, and why has he targeted Paige?"

"I wouldn't know." Gentry proved suitably aloof, giving a weak shrug. "But don't look at me. I've been off and on conference calls with various vendors since six this morning. Isn't that right, Eli?"

That brought an uneasy look from Eli. "I know it was early. I arrived around seven fifteen, and you were already here."

"There you go." His tone was smug. "Now, if you don't have any other questions, I need to get back. I have some replica art pieces I'm trying to negotiate. And the longer I'm gone, the less leverage I have."

Seth felt his patience—the little that he had left— wither. "Sorry, Gentry. I actually stopped by about something else."

Gentry grunted a low sigh. "Okay, Garrison, what is it now?"

With frustration knotting his throat, Seth shifted his weight, eager to get this show going. "Yesterday you mentioned you weren't sure if Trey was aware of the family trust."

"That's enough." The smugness on Gentry's face evaporated, and he looked at Seth stiffly. "I really prefer not to discuss family or financial matters publicly. If you need specific details about my personal business, you can talk to my attorney."

Seth scratched his cheek, confused. Why would Gentry be so protective of the trust fund? If anything, Trey being beneficiary at the time of Madison's death gave the charges against him even more credibility. Something wasn't right here.

"Gentry, I don't have time to talk to your attorney," Seth said, making a production of looking at his watch. "It's late in the day, and our timeline is short, so why don't you ask old Eli here to take a hike so we can talk privately. Or maybe we just need to take a trip downtown."

"This is ridiculous." Gentry just looked at Seth, nostrils flaring. Then Seth noticed the slight sag of his shoulders as he seemed to ponder Seth's words. With a dramatic sigh, Gentry motioned for Eli to leave. "Please go let Mr. Wong know that I'll call him back later. And then get yourself something to eat."

"Are you sure you don't need me?" Eli's thick eyebrows knit.

"I'm good," Gentry said.

"All right." Eli turned and walked down the hallway.

Good. Gentry looked ready to talk. It saved Seth the paperwork of having to make an arrest and drag him downtown.

Gentry swung his gaze to Seth and started out as poignant as ever. "Listen up, Garrison. I never even knew anything about Trey being added as beneficiary until after Madison's death."

"So Madison never told you." Seth scratched his head. "And the executor never mentioned it?"

"Correct," Gentry said firmly. "He's bound by laws, too, and he couldn't divulge that kind of information without Madison's permission. And apparently Madison asked him not to inform me."

"And why wouldn't she want you to know?"

Gentry looked at Seth oddly, as if the answer was clear. "Because I wouldn't have been in favor of it."

Seth nodded, trying to figure Gentry out. A man who liked control. So much so that his sister hid information from him. Seth thought again about Trey and Madison's elopement. Was Madison's impulsivity a coping skill to avoid her brother's control?

This family Seth once thought of as close-knit was starting to look more frayed at the seams.

"Okay, Gentry." Seth placed his hands on his hips. "I don't want to get into the family drama between you and your sister, but I don't understand why, after you found out Trey had been named beneficiary, you didn't inform the detectives. This kind of information would only add to suspicion of his guilt."

"If Trey's lawyers found out their client had millions of dollars on the line, they'd be making up evidence to get the guy off," Gentry blurted with a sudden flush of annoyance. "Everybody knows money talks. And attorneys spend more time on clients with money."

Wow. That was quite a theory. One Gentry had obviously put some thought into. "You mustn't have much faith in the legal system."

"Nope. None," Gentry said with conviction. That explained a lot, Seth thought. Like why he had no respect for law enforcement in general. "Don't you watch the news? Guilty people get off all the time."

And innocent people went to jail. Seth eased against the wooden porch post and crossed his arms. Interesting perspective. One that had him wondering about the evidence in Trey's case. Had it been planted as a way to frame Trey? And if so, was Gentry involved?

"So." Seth cleared his throat. "Do you think Madison's money played any part in her murder?"

Gentry said nothing for a moment. He shifted slightly, stuffing his hands in his sweat jacket pockets. "Actually, no. I think Trey is just crazy. My sister didn't want to be married, and he just couldn't accept that."

"So why, then, would you think someone would want to kill Amy? Madison's best friend?"

Gentry didn't bother to think about that. He looked Seth hard in the eye and said, "How would I know? You're the detective, Detective."

Ignoring his attempt at sarcasm, Seth scratched his head. "It just makes me wonder what Amy might have known that someone would be willing to kill over."

Gentry lifted his chin. "Amy's dead, Detective. So I guess that's something we'll never know."

"I'm thinking about reopening Madison's murder investigation."

"What? You can't be serious." Brett shifted to the edge of the couch, nearly spilling his coffee, his body rigid as a scowl narrowed his face. "Why open that can of worms when we still have so little to go on?"

Paige walked into Seth's living room from the kitchen and was taken aback. As much as she was both surprised and elated by Seth's statement, her stomach curdled at Brett's hostile reaction. As her brother's close friend, shouldn't he be receptive to reopening a case that could possibly help prove Trey innocent?

Paige quietly eased into a seat at the opposite end of the sofa from Brett, knowing this wasn't the best time to voice her opinion.

Seth rose from his chair and started to pace, the heels of his boots thudding against the hardwood. "I really think we should reopen Madison's case, now that we have Amy's preliminary autopsy report deeming her death a homicide. Somebody killed her to keep her quiet. About what, we don't know. But she was Madison's best friend and had doubts about Trey being Madison's killer."

Paige's heart stopped. The autopsy report was news to her. Although what she'd expected, it was still an awful revelation, but one she hoped would help the case against her brother.

But Brett wasn't so easily convinced. "I don't think that's enough of a reason," he shot back and then began stating his case as to why it was best to leave Madison's murder investigation alone. Although he didn't directly mention Trey, the reality was that Trey would remain the prime suspect.

The dinner in Paige's stomach tumbled into a tight knot.

"I could understand you going that route," Brett continued, "if we didn't suspect Paige's attacks to be a vengeful act committed by someone looking for revenge against Trey. Amy was unfortunately a casualty of that someone's paranoia. The guy is getting nervous, impulsive. He needs to be stopped before he gets to Paige or hurts someone else he thinks may suspect him."

Paige shifted on the sofa. On that one note she agreed with Brett. Her attacker—Amy's killer—was impulsive. Who knew what he'd try next. Still, her focus was to link him to Madison's murder. She only wished she could convince Brett.

Seth stopped short and looked at Brett. "That's a great scenario, but like you said, there are too many unknowns to bank on anything conclusive yet."

The tension in the room inched up a notch, radiating between Seth and Brett like a high-voltage line.

Brett sat up straighter, his face set in hard lines. "We have to have a direction to go in or we'll get nothing accomplished. But before I start tangling what we know

now with the evidence connected to Trey, I need to see some hard facts. Until then, I have my eye on Gentry for Paige's attacks. He's angry about his sister's murder, and Paige coming back to town probably amped him up even more and pushed him to the brink of trying to kill her. And we both know that guilt breeds paranoia. My guess is everyone he worked with knew his feelings about Trey and also his annoyance at Paige being back in town. When he saw Amy talking to Paige, he blew a gasket. He was worried about something. Maybe worried that Amy suspected he ran Paige off the road. It doesn't seem like he kept his hatred for Trey a secret. It makes sense, and I plan to continue running my investigation to that effect."

Seth stared at Brett from across the room. "And you don't think Gentry could have killed his sister? Remember, there was a trust fund at stake."

Brett shook his head and clunked the mug he was holding on the coffee table. "At this point, no."

What if Gentry was Madison's killer? Paige's jaw dropped, unable to believe what she was hearing. Brett was so eager to dismiss a trust fund, but wouldn't let go of the evidence stacked up against her brother. Yet he was speculating scenarios for the recent events where there was also no firm evidence. Why did she ever think he'd be willing to help her? "Brett..." Her throat threatened to close, and her heart ceased to beat. "I can't believe you wouldn't give my brother the benefit of the doubt and at least consider the possibility that he was set up. By Gentry or someone else."

That brought both Seth's and Brett's eyes back on her.

"Paige, I'm sorry," Brett said after a moment. "I just can't ignore the evidence we already have against Trey. And trying to *disprove* it and then connect Gentry to Madison's murder sounds to me like a complicated, futile venture at this point. One that could cost us weeks. And we can't afford to lose time running on wild-goose chases, not with a murderer still on the loose."

What? A bad feeling gathered in her midsection, spiking her adrenaline. So was Brett saying he was willing to sacrifice her brother's life out of convenience? She sat up ramrod straight. "Brett—"

"Paige," Seth gently cut her off.

Paige swung her gaze to meet his, and the look he shot her said, *I've got this.* The tension bunching her muscles started to dissipate.

Relieved, Paige settled back in her seat. Finally, an advocate for her brother.

"Brett, I disagree," Seth started, hands on his hips. Paige could feel a standoff brewing. "I think you're not giving Gentry enough credit for what he could be capable of. For years Gentry controlled everything. The family business. The trust. Madison. And then Madison grew up and wanted control of her life and her own money. So much so she makes her husband her trust fund's beneficiary and keeps it a secret from her brother. And as type A as Gentry is, he didn't find out accidentally. He made it his business to know her business."

"So Gentry might have set up my brother," Paige blurted before she could stop herself. Trying to fit the pieces together. "Because if Trey was the beneficiary and is convicted—"

"He wouldn't get a cent," Seth said, catching her gaze. "And the money stays with the family."

"Wow, that's a great scenario," Brett said as he stood. "And you almost had me sold, but you're still forgetting about a mountain of evidence stacked against Trey. A better scenario, in my opinion, is Trey didn't want the divorce, and losing Madison and all her money pushed him over the edge."

Paige ground her teeth. Frustration didn't even begin to describe what she was feeling about Brett's *better scenario*.

A shrug preceded Seth's words. "I used to see it from that perspective, but now I think that both scenarios need to be explored."

"Then you better get on it." Brett huffed and started for the door, then just as quickly turned back and pointed a finger at Seth. "Please help me understand one thing before I go. You were Trey's arresting officer and saw every shred of evidence linking him to Madison's murder, and even declared him the only suspect. But now you think *you* might have been wrong and he might be innocent?"

There was cold silence, stretching painfully long before Seth finally answered the question. "Yes, Brett. It is a possibility that I might have been wrong about Trey."

Paige's heart stopped before it jolted into a jubilant cha-cha. Ten long months and finally the words she'd longed to hear. She wanted nothing more than to jump from her seat and swing her arms around Seth in a big hug. A friendly hug, of course, but she stopped herself. Hardly appropriate. She fought back a sigh.

"I think you're heading down the wrong road with this, Seth," Brett came back. The scowl on his face nudged her annoyance to a new level. "And I personally don't have time for it."

Seth shrugged, suggesting he was more relieved than disappointed. "I'm doing what I think needs to be done. I'll keep you posted as I find out more."

"In the meantime, I'll be focusing on Gentry and his ties to Paige's attacks and Amy's death. I'm not going back ten months on this one," Brett firmly stated and then looked at Paige. "You know how to reach me if you need something."

She didn't acknowledge him. She wouldn't be calling. Instead, Paige looked at Seth as Brett finally walked out the door. "Have you really changed your opinion on my brother's guilt?"

An uneasy look crossed Seth's face, and he hesitated as if he didn't want to commit to anything yet. "Like I said to Brett, it makes sense to do some investigating on how Madison's murder ties in to your attacks and Amy's murder. Just in case the same person is responsible for all three. So, I guess you can say I'm keeping an open mind."

And she was thrilled. She gave an approving smile. "So what's next on your agenda, Detective?"

Seth crossed his arms over his chest. "Tomorrow morning we head to Durham."

"Durham?"

"I need to talk to Trey."

Uh-oh. Seth's idea had Paige chewing the inside of her cheek. She hadn't mentioned to Trey that she'd come back to Boone. Nor did she plan to. Not with a killer hot on her heels as she tried to dig up evidence to help him.

Nope. This was not cool.

A small voice inside her reiterated that—one that sensed Trey's reaction, whispering, *Not a good idea.* She hoped she was wrong.

EIGHT

At seven the next morning, Seth climbed into the cab of his truck to start the three-hour journey to the Durham County Jail. While Paige had been rather quiet since she got up, he could see appreciation in her eyes for his effort to help Trey.

It warmed his heart deeply to be helping her now. Walking this journey alone had to be difficult. He only wished he been there for her all along. Even more, he wished he could rewrite the history between them.

But one look in Paige's eyes and the sorrow lingering there and he knew nothing would ever be the same between them. Once this was all over, she'd walk out of Boone and never look back. And he wouldn't blame her.

"Do you really think going all the way to Durham is necessary?" Paige asked, buckling up. "With his trial still slated for next week, is that the best use of our time? I don't think he can tell you any more than I already have."

"No, I have questions that only he can answer." Seth cranked the engine and shifted into gear, then started down the pocked and rutted driveway. He needed to talk to Trey face-to-face. See his expressions. Look in his eyes. The last time he'd spoken to Trey, he was anything but himself. Distraught. Angry. A poor historian when it came to Madison's murder. Maybe now, ten months later, he could shed some light on what really happened that night.

He only hoped his gut feeling had pushed him on the right track. He kept asking himself if he'd be making this trip if it hadn't been for Paige's persistence that her brother was innocent. He'd like to say yes, but, truthfully, he wasn't sure. There was a lot of evidence to disprove—fingerprints, DNA, murder weapon—all with Trey's name engraved on it. Still, someone cunning with an agenda could have orchestrated the perfect crime. And for that niggling *maybe*, he needed to talk to Trey. Give him one more chance to clear his name.

"I'm sure your brother will be happy to see you." He cast Paige a sideways glance. "Although I get the impression that you're not too excited to see him."

Paige slumped deeper into the seat, crossing her arms over her chest. "No—no, I'm always happy to see Trey."

He didn't buy her cool response. "But…"

"But what?" She looked his way, catching his glance.

Seth dropped her a knowing smile and then pulled his eyes back on the road. "Trey doesn't know you came to Boone, does he?"

"Well, actually…no," she said after a moment as they turned onto Highway 421, heading west. "I didn't want him to be concerned. He already has enough on his plate."

Trey did have enough on his plate, and Seth could only imagine what he was going through; waiting for a court date couldn't be easy. But Seth felt better knowing that Paige's return to Boone was not at her brother's request. And given the vibes he was getting from Paige, Trey wasn't going to be happy to hear about his sister's attempt to help him. Especially if he knew that she'd been putting her life on the line since she'd been in town.

Paige rested her hand on his arm, and he flinched in surprise. It had been a long time since she'd reacted so comfortably around him. And he had to admit it felt good. "By the way, thank you for all you're doing to help Trey."

A hint of a smile pulled at Seth's lips. He was starting to see the old Paige again. "You're welcome. But I'm just doing my job. Like I told you before, if ever evidence popped up that brought Trey's guilt into question, I wouldn't ignore it."

"You're a man of your word, and I appreciate that."

Despite being concerned for her safety, Seth admired her passion and integrity. Although his heart skipped a beat, he knew mending fences with her would be difficult. And honestly, he wasn't sure they could ever see past their negative history.

His cell phone rang, and he hit the button on his Bluetooth headset. "This is Seth Garrison."

"Hey, Seth, it's Ted."

"Ted, what do you know?" Something good, he hoped.

"I found a couple things about Gentry I thought might be of interest."

"As long as it involves a trust fund or murder, I'm all ears."

Ted laughed. "Not specifically, but close. It seems Gentry's been having some financial issues."

"Really?" Seth ran his hand along the steering wheel, his interest piqued.

"It began a couple years ago, after he started dabbling in the foreign market, importing high-end pieces of art and other merchandise."

"I'm sure that's volatile. So was he a little overzealous with purchases or did he just make some bad investments?"

"Not sure, maybe both. But he did file for bankruptcy

protection about this time last year and then retracted it a month later."

"That was right before Madison's murder," Seth muttered more to himself than to Ted.

"Yeah. I found that interesting, too."

"Do you know if Gentry's blown the funds from his trust?"

"Not sure, but working on finding out. But, for now, hopefully we've got enough to get those rusty wheels in your head going."

Oh, yeah. The wheels in his head were already busy churning up possible scenarios. All of which included Gentry and cast doubt on Trey's guilt. "Thanks, Ted. Good work and keep it coming."

Seth disconnected and looked at Paige. "I think I feel progress."

She gave a strained smile, apparently not sharing his optimism. "I'm glad, because progress still feels a long way off to me."

"You okay?"

She nodded, smoothed her hair from her face and heaved an exhausted sigh. "As I was sitting here, it hit me that Trey's trial is in less than a week. Mentally, I get that, but I think emotionally it's just sinking in. I feel at such a loss, for myself and my brother. I just wish I could do more to help him."

At her raw sentiment Seth's heart broke in two. He wished he could tell her everything would be okay, but he couldn't. "I've never seen a greater advocate than you, Paige. Your brother should be proud. Because I'm very proud of you."

Paige remained quiet for a long moment. Finally she murmured, "Thank you."

"You're welcome," he said, feeling her sorrow. Her

fear. A wave of sadness engulfed him and just as fast, guilt.

"What's the chance..." She stopped, the strain in her voice evident as she shifted in her seat to look at him. "If you do proceed and reopen the murder investigation, will that be enough to put Trey's trial on hold?" Another difficult question he couldn't answer. Nothing in life was ever that simple.

"It wouldn't be automatic, if that is what you're asking. Any new evidence would have to be presented to Trey's attorneys. So, ultimately it will be up to them to petition the court to reschedule or, in the best-case scenario, have the charges against Trey dropped. But unless we can prove beyond a reasonable doubt that Trey isn't guilty, the trial will likely go on as planned." And Trey's fate would be left in the jury's hands.

"So our time crunch continues."

"Yes, it does." Seth gripped the cool leather of the steering wheel. The reality was, time continued to tick by faster than clues were coming in. They still had a daunting task ahead of them. And given the evidence against Trey, things didn't look good. But Seth stayed mum on that subject, deciding to remain optimistic that if Trey truly was innocent, they'd find what they needed to prove it.

Sometimes impossible dreams came true. And for Paige's sake, he hoped this one did.

Three hours and four pit stops later, Seth took a right off the highway, and the five-story, monolithic white building came into view.

Low clouds hung overhead, casting an oppressive shadow over the jail.

Swallowing tightly, Seth glanced at Paige, who was staring out the windshield, all expression wiped from her face. He could sense her discomfort, her worry. Gripping the steering wheel tighter, he resisted the urge to reach out and take her hand. To offer her comfort.

Get a grip, Garrison. Keep your emotions out of it, he firmly reminded himself.

Seth shook off those feelings and maneuvered his truck through two massive stone gates, where the tree-lined road gave way to a narrow, desolate street, barren except for the strategically placed sky-high industrial lights.

He parked in the visitor section, and they climbed out and headed across the parking lot. But Seth noticed the closer they came to the check-in center, the slower Paige's pace became.

"Are you okay?" Seth glanced at her, finding a bewildered look on her face.

Paige bobbed her head. "It takes a few minutes to psych myself up for this. You'd think that after all this time I'd be used to it. But I still don't have a warm and fuzzy feeling about this place."

"Actually, that's probably a good thing." Seth grinned at her. "Just relax, I'm right here with you." He hoped that offered her some comfort and not added anxiety.

But when a slight smile danced across her lips, his heart skipped a beat.

Once inside, they went through the check-in process: passed through the metal detector, showed ID and surrendered their personal items—wallets, cell phones, keys, anything that could be construed as contraband. Then they were finally escorted to a no-contact visiting booth to wait for Trey.

While they sat there, Paige stayed silent, hands clasped in her lap. She stared dully through the Plexiglas divider, waiting for Trey to be brought in. Seth knew she was hurting and exhausted, but even more so, a fighter.

Gloom settled like a wool blanket on his shoulders when he thought about what they were up against. Keeping Paige safe was still his top concern. The harder they dug for the truth, the more desperate Paige's stalker would become. But desperation bred mistakes and mistakes opportunity. Unfortunately, a lot could happen before then.

After a few minutes, Trey was led in by a guard. He moved slowly with a shuffling gait, his posture hunched, body stiff. He was shackled and handcuffed, wearing an orange jumpsuit. A man broken, and yet, Seth could still see the warrior in him. Strong and determined, a familiar trait, and like his sister, a fighter.

The guard unlocked Trey's cuffs and then walked out, the metal door clanging shut behind him. Trey didn't even try to make eye contact until he dropped into the lone plastic chair and picked up the handset.

Paige was ready, holding the visitation phone in a death grip in her hand.

Seth stood in the background, giving Paige a moment to talk to her brother.

As Paige pressed the handset to her ear, Trey's narrowed gaze shifted over her shoulder and landed on Seth. "What's he doing here?"

Seth didn't need a handset to make out his words. Nor did he miss the disgust on his face. There had been a lot of tense moments following Trey's arrest, leaving their once strong relationship in shambles.

Paige leaned in. "Seth is here to talk to you about some possible new evidence."

"Evidence?" Trey's gaze shifted back to Paige.

"I'll let Seth explain." Paige handed Seth the handset.

"Trey, I hope you're doing okay."

Trey didn't respond. But his cold stare could have scorched through metal.

"Trey, I know this is awkward," Seth said, already feeling the tension radiating through the Plexiglas between them. "But we've come across some new information and I'd like to ask you a couple questions."

Trey lifted a shoulder in a shrug, his mouth softening into a less hostile frown. "Okay."

Slipping down into the chair beside Paige, Seth hoped getting eye to eye with Trey might help ease some of the tension. "We recently gained information regarding the Cramers' family trust. Could you tell me what you know about Madison's share?"

A bewildered expression crossed Trey's face, giving Seth the answer he needed. "A trust fund? As in family money?" Trey said after a moment.

Seth nodded.

Trey shook his head, a wary look in his eyes. "I never heard anything about a trust fund."

Seth leaned in closer. "Are you sure there was never even a hint from any of the Cramer family members? Because each one—Madison, her mother and brother—received a fairly substantial settlement after Frank Cramer's death."

Trey shifted on the molded plastic seat, shaking his head. "No, I never heard a peep from anyone. Are you sure it's even true?"

Seth exchanged a look with Paige, who gave him an encouraging smile. He looked back at Trey. "It's not idle hearsay, it's been confirmed. Rubin Avery is the trust executor. Ever hear of him?"

Trey thought for a moment then shook his head. "No, never heard of the guy," he said, his dark brows pulling into a tight frown over his eyes. "But it still doesn't make sense. Madison and I were always hurting for money. Madison liked nice things. She spent money faster than we could make it. And lack of money was the source of a lot of our arguments."

Trey looked confused and more than a little alarmed that the relationship he remembered was actually based on lies. Seth was confused himself. Madison's lack of trust in people must have kept her from telling Trey. And although she'd made a bold decision to add Trey as beneficiary, she might not have had the nerve to request draws from her trust until after they'd separated. That was when it appeared she had finally decided to stop using her brother as intermediary between her and the trust executor. A gutsy move, pulling away from her brother's control. And Seth could only imagine what Gentry thought about that.

Seth continued. "Did you notice Madison having more access to money after you separated?"

"I don't know," Trey said with a limp shrug. "I wasn't around her enough. The last text I received from her was the day she died, asking me to stop by so we could talk. That was the first time I'd heard from her in weeks. We had agreed not to talk for a month and then reconvene and discuss where our future was headed."

He stared off blankly, anguish and despair clearly stamped on his face as he continued recounting the last communication he'd had with Madison. The last day of her life. He was rambling, but Seth let him talk. "When she contacted me and wanted to talk before our agreed-upon date, I knew then that we were done." Trey shook his head, suddenly looking exhausted. Broken. Like the wind had been kicked out of him.

On that day, the feeling of loss must have overwhelmed him, pushing him into a valley of despair. He'd relapsed that day. And the relationship he'd feared losing had been ripped apart in the most brutal way by Madison's murder.

Seth felt Paige's hand on his arm, and when he glanced at her he saw tears in her eyes. Seth swallowed, understanding. This was an emotional moment for everyone.

Trey visibly sighed and straightened in his seat with what appeared to be determined composure. "Sorry about this." He plowed his hands through his short hair. "I try not to think about Madison, and this is why."

Seth could relate. Thinking about a lost love was never productive, but unfortunately necessary in this instance. He pressed on. "What about Gentry? Did he and Madison get along?"

Trey shrugged. "They had their issues like everyone else but for the most part got along."

"What were their issues?"

Leaning in, Trey propped one elbow on the counter. "Gentry liked to give advice, and Madison didn't like to take it. Just like my little sister." He cocked a dark eyebrow at Paige, and Seth couldn't miss his knowing expression. Trey didn't want Paige involved in his case.

She returned a sheepish grin. Obviously not having trouble keeping up with the conversation.

"Was his advice about money?" Seth continued.

Trey shrugged again. "I don't know. Madison didn't give specifics, just grumbled about him not thinking she was capable of making her own decisions."

A thousand questions whirled in Seth's mind about the dynamics of the Cramer household. *Power. Money. Control.* But, in consideration of time, he didn't want to open that can of worms. Instead he directed his focus to Gentry's personal issues.

"If any of the Cramers had access to big money, they never let on," Trey said, scratching his head. "In fact

Gentry had a couple bad investments. You'd think if he had the funds—"

Bingo. That's what Seth was waiting for. "What kind of bad investments?" he interrupted.

Trey settled back against the molded white chair and folded his arms. "Work related is all I know. But…" He sat up straight again, as if a lightbulb had just gone off in his head. "If you're thinking Gentry murdered Madison, I think you're off base. He might have been a little controlling, but he cared about Madison and her well-being."

Trey was a bigger man than most. This was his opportunity to shift blame, and yet he refused to sacrifice someone else in hopes of saving himself.

"There are a lot of things in life that surprise us. And sometimes it involves the people we least expect." Seth switched the handset to the other ear. "But no concrete conclusions have been made yet. Is there anything else you could tell us about the night Madison was murdered?"

"I didn't do it." Trey's gaze caught his, a challenging stare. "But that hasn't changed since the day you arrested me and charged me with murder. So my question to you, Garrison, is why, after ten months, are you trying to help me?"

Seth thought for a moment, wondering how much he should divulge about what had been going on. Paige gave him a sharp little nudge with her elbow, as if to say, *don't do it.* He cleared his throat. "New evidence turned up. I can't ignore it."

Trey only nodded, silent for a moment. "Are you two—" his pointed finger swayed between Seth and Paige "—back together?"

"No," they both said in unison. Apparently Paige was as uncomfortable about the question as he was, and unlike him, there was not an inkling of remorse in her answer.

Paige grabbed the handset. "I know we don't have much more time, so how have you been doing?"

Trey didn't miss her attempt to circumvent the direction of the conversation. He shook his head, edging closer to the dividing window. Seth watched carefully, reading his lips. "You and Seth aren't dating again, but you came here together? Are you back in Boone?"

"No. I mean, yes. Temporarily," Paige stammered, her face practically bloodless, pale as chalk.

"That's what I was afraid of." Trey firmed his jaw and shook his head. "Give the phone back to Garrison."

Paige hesitated a second, then at Trey's second request, she turned the handset over to Seth. And the dark look she gave him said not to elaborate, but something told Seth Trey already had it figured out.

"Garrison, I read in the paper about the recent murder in Boone and that the killer is still at large and also suspected of making attempts on another woman's life. Please tell me Paige isn't involved in this."

Seth hesitated and took a deep breath. "I'm sorry, Trey—"

That's as far as he got before Trey pushed back his chair and rose, a vivid flush filling his face. "That's what I thought." His gaze jumped to Paige. "Don't do this." He pointed at her. "Don't try to be a hero to save me. Some people get a raw deal in life. Don't waste your life trying to figure it out. It's my problem, not yours." Trey's voice cracked with emotion before it trailed off.

Seth was glad it was him holding the line and not Paige. The emotion in Trey's voice was almost too much for Seth.

Paige grabbed the handset from him, fresh tears glinting at her brother's obvious distress. "Trey, I want to help you. I won't sit by and let you take the hit for a crime you didn't commit. Just like you'd do for me if our situation was reversed."

Paige's rationale fell on deaf ears. "Paige, please listen to me and just back off."

Before Paige could disagree, Trey hung the handset back in its cradle. He turned to summon the guard.

Paige jumped to her feet. "Trey! Don't leave!" She screamed into the phone. But Trey couldn't hear her through the soundproof barrier.

The door slammed as he exited the room with the guard.

Seth's gut clenched at the sound of Paige's sobs. He drew her into his arms, holding her tight as she cried against his chest.

"Trey is going to trial in a few days. And now... because of me, he has more stress to deal with."

Instinctively, Seth tightened his embrace, hoping to calm her, to make her feel safe. At the same time trying to ignore how overwhelmingly right it felt to have her back in his arms. After all this was over, she would be gone; he knew that without a shadow of doubt. There were too many unpleasant memories in Boone. "Are you ready to step aside and let me take over?"

"No," she whispered against his chest. "Even if Trey wants me to, I can't give up on him. I want your help, Seth, but I'm not leaving."

Her action was a true testament of her loyalty and unwavering belief in her brother's innocence. And he planned to walk this road with her. Because more and more he was thinking she might be right.

Feeling Seth's glances throughout the ride home, Paige knew he wanted to talk. If not about the case then probably light chatter about anything that would make the long trip go by quicker. But she was exhausted. Both mentally and emotionally.

She couldn't stop thinking about her brother and the worry and pain in his eyes when he'd learned what she'd been up to. Her heart constricted from sadness as she thought about inflicting any more pain in his life.

He'd always been there for her; why couldn't he just accept her wanting to help him?

The answer was simple, and she knew it. He was worried about her safety, just like Seth was. She got that, but still, somebody had to help Trey. And she'd come too far to turn back now. Seth was finally committed to doing what he could. She could never repay him for all he'd done. She prayed a silent prayer for Seth. For his safety and that God would direct her and him to the truth. That prayer stayed on her lips.

Settling back against the seat, Paige closed her eyes and tried to tune out Seth's voice as he chatted with Ted on the phone. She was grateful for the distraction for Seth, and hopefully what they were discussing would help her brother's case.

Even as Paige tried to rest, the three-hour ride felt more like six. Her mind just wouldn't let go, racing instead in a thousand different directions. But even as her brain scurried for ideas, she knew that evidence against Gentry was what they needed. And it was going to take some digging on Seth's part to accomplish that.

Finally, around two they arrived back at the cabin. As Paige double-checked the locks on the front door of the cabin, she watched Seth's truck disappear down the driveway. Just when she thought she was over him, old feelings of affection crowded her heart. Biting her lip to keep burning tears at bay, she shook her head. She needed to accept that some things just weren't meant to be.

And she and Seth were one.

Still, she couldn't help but love this man for stepping up to the plate to keep her safe. And now he was off to Cramer's Antiques to talk to the employees about Madison's and Amy's murders. One place she never cared to step foot in again.

Fortunately, being a detective gave him more clout in asking questions and gathering information, unlike her blundering attempts, which got her nowhere—except inadvertently landing her in jail—and provoked someone to murder Amy. She bit her lip. If only she'd had five more minutes to talk to Amy. What intuitions did Amy have? About Madison's murder or Paige's attacks?

Suddenly chilled to the bone, Paige shivered. That was something they'd never know.

Pushing aside her frustration, Paige wandered down the hall to the kitchen. Ruby was up in her room and Laser caught up with Paige, barking and dancing in circles around her feet.

"Shh, Laser." She squatted down beside him, scratching between his ears. "Quiet, buddy. Miss Ruby's asleep." But he kept barking, his body fidgeting, his tail wildly banging the wood banister.

"He's been acting like that for the last hour," Ruby said from the top of the stairs. "I guess he just missed you."

"I'm sorry he woke you." Paige glanced up the stairs. "He's probably out of his element and antsy with so many visitors in the house." Something she could relate to herself.

"Probably." Ruby laughed. Tucking her book under her arm, she started down the staircase. "I was about to make some tea. Care to join me?"

Tea did sound wonderful. "Sure, I'll be right there after I let Laser out. Maybe that's what he wants."

"Okay, I'll grab the box of mint tea."

As Ruby walked out of the entry, Paige opened the door, and Laser shot out. *When nature calls*... Paige laughed and then headed into the kitchen, leaving all worries of Trey's upcoming trial and her stalker tucked in the back of her mind. She was in a safe haven and Seth was now in charge, so for the moment she willed herself to relax. And a hot mug of mint tea would definitely help with that.

Seth turned onto the highway, glad Paige had agreed to stay at the cabin with his mother. Seeing her brother had taken a toll on her and hopefully she'd get some rest. Besides, what he had to attend to was something he needed to do alone.

A couple miles down the road, Seth slowed to a stop behind a row of vehicles waiting at the rail crossing for a freight train to pass. As he sat there, drumming his fingers on the steering wheel, his mind bounced through several scenarios.

With so much seemingly irrefutable evidence against Trey, pulling Gentry into the suspect spotlight would be futile. Brett was right about that. Without concrete evidence, they'd have a hard time convincing the judge and jury.

Then again, even if his gut suspected that Trey had been framed for Madison's murder, who was to say Gentry wasn't now being set up to take the heat for crimes he hadn't committed? One red flag about Gentry was his behavior. His cocky personality and bad attitude were not easily missed. Unlike the pleasant demeanor he wore around town, he'd put out zero effort in trying to impress Seth or anyone else in law enforcement.

He was almost begging to be investigated. Was it because he was innocent and there was nothing to hide? Or did he think he was smarter than the average investigator and enjoyed watching them scramble, only to run into brick walls?

A psychopath's dream. But was that psychopath Gentry?

Okay. Enough. Seth took a deep breath, refocusing on the facts they did have. Like the ballistic report from yesterday's shooting. Ted had finally gotten his hands on a preliminary draft, which answered a lot of Seth's questions. He wasn't surprised to learn the shells found at the scene belonged to a Remington 870—a popular hunting shotgun, and in these parts, about as common as the extended-cab white truck they were *still* looking for.

Which served to remind Seth what they were dealing with. A cold and deliberate, methodical killer.

The last of the railcars passed. The clanging bell stopped sounding, and the train-crossing bars started to rise. He drove over the tracks, heading south down the highway toward Cramer's Antiques. He needed to dig a little deeper into Gentry's background, and what better character references than his employees?

As promised, he put a call in to Brett, giving him the heads-up on his plans and also his conversation with Trey. And funny thing, Brett stayed mum on any strides he'd made in the investigation. Seth almost laughed. So much for crime-fighting partners working together—which was why he'd enlisted Ted's help in tracking down leads and figuring out the depth of Gentry's financial issues. Ted was a man he could trust.

If he didn't know better, he might wonder about Brett and what ulterior motive he might have to see Trey convicted of Madison's murder. Brett had been Trey's friend, so why wouldn't he be pushing to reopen the investigation? Was he that convinced of Trey's guilt, or was there something more devious going on?

Seth squashed that last thought. He hated when his brain tried to overreason. Brett was Brett. Stubborn, opinionated, but a good detective. He was focused on Paige's case and who was behind trying to kill her. And Seth couldn't discount that. They needed all the help they could get.

The bell over the door jingled as Seth walked into Cramer's Antiques. He gave the place a quick scan. It was almost like a museum with its cluttered displays of old and new knickknacks, vintage jewelry and books, and even specialty food items and plants, which were mixed in amid scores of antique furniture.

Gingerly, he stepped past one of the displays to the old hardwood bar that served as the checkout counter. He took another look around, noticing a sign overhead pointing to the art gallery in the back of the store. As far as merchandise went, this place had it all. Other than that, there wasn't a person in sight. Not a clerk. Not a customer. Silent.

Seth was just about to venture toward the back of the store when he heard a slight rustling to his left and then the sound of somebody clearing their throat.

Stepping forward, Seth peered between two display shelves and saw Eli in the corner of the room unloading a large cardboard box of imported chocolate. Perfect. Just the man he wanted to see.

"Good afternoon, Eli," he said walking his way.

Eli looked up and glanced at Seth, nearly losing his grip on the box he was holding. A flash of alarm flared in his eyes, only fleeting but enough to rouse Seth's suspicions. Maybe Amy wasn't the only employee with reservations about talking about their bosses, the Cramers.

Which made Seth wonder what kind of fear-based workplace Gentry ran. Oddly enough, in Eli's case, it was one that seemed to foster employee loyalty.

"What can I do for you, Mr. Garrison?" Eli went back to setting out the boxes on the display. The loyal employee playing it cool.

Seth came up beside him. "Wow, this is some place. I never would have guessed the variety of merchandise that was here."

"Yeah, we try to cover our bases. Carry a little bit of everything." Eli gestured with the box in his hand. "We're in the middle of our afternoon lull, so if you'd like to do a little shopping, Sarah is here somewhere and she can show you what we've got."

"I appreciate that," Seth said, making a point to look around. "However, I actually stopped by to ask a few questions."

"Sorry, Mr. Cramer isn't here."

"That's fine. If you have a moment, I'd actually like to talk to you."

Eli hesitated and then shrugged. "I guess I have a few minutes."

"Good." Seth smiled at him. "So, how long have you worked for the Cramers?"

Eli took out several more boxes of chocolate. "Twelve years. I grew up working here. Like most of the employees here, I started in my teens."

"Must be a good place to work," Seth said as he reached for a small cast-iron pig on a shelf. "So, you knew the family well? Madison, her mother."

"Yes. And Mr. Cramer when he was alive. Great people."

Seth fingered the pig figurine in his hand, surprised by its weight. But he was even more surprised when he turned it over and saw the price. *Who buys this stuff?* Shaking his head, he set it back down. "I guess you know this business well. And now you're, what? Gentry's right-hand guy?"

Eli stopped stacking a moment and shrugged. "You can say that."

"So is business going good?" Seth stepped closer. "I know it takes a lot of finesse to run a business like this. Dealing with a variety of vendors, trying to keep on top of the market and working to get the right prices."

"It's a job you have to pay close attention to. Big gains and big losses are part of the game. Sometimes it can be like a roller-coaster ride."

"I'm sure you're right." Seth scratched his head. "So where would you say Cramer's Antiques is on that roller coaster?"

Eli stopped and stared at Seth, suddenly looking self-conscious. "It's not really my place to say, Mr. Garrison."

"Are you aware if Gentry was having any financial issues?"

"I'm not privy to Gentry's personal finances."

Seth didn't miss a beat. "How about Madison? Did she ever confide in you?"

"About her finances?"

Seth shrugged. "About anything. Issues with her husband? Issues with her brother?"

As if reading his mind, a muscle ticked in Eli's jaw and he stood stock-still, hands on his hips. "I tried to be cordial to you, Mr. Garrison, but I can see that our conversation is going nowhere. If you're trying to set up Gentry to take the heat for Madison's murder, you'll have to get your dirt from some other source."

Seth wasn't that easily deterred, so he threw in, "How

about the recent attacks on Paige? Do you think Gentry could have been involved?"

Eli dropped his arms and squared his shoulders. Full-on attack mode. The man had perfected his intimidator role. "I'm sorry about what's been going on with Miss Becker, but I have no information that can help you."

Seth knew a dead end when he saw one. Eli had shut down. Which was okay—Seth had gotten his message across, that he had his eye on Gentry, and if Gentry had any doubt before about how seriously he was being looked at, he'd know now.

In the truck, before Seth even cranked the engine, his phone vibrated. He reached for his pocket and pulled it out. It was Ted. "Hey, buddy, tell me something good."

"I think you might want to make a trip down to the station." Ted's voice held a serious tone.

Sounded promising already. Seth straightened up. "What do you have?"

"A couple out on a walk this morning found a discarded shotgun in the woods beside the condo complex. It's a Winchester Model 70."

"No kidding." Things were looking up. "Have forensics gotten a hold of it yet?"

"Yes. It's a perfect match to bullets that were fired at the condo unit. And they were able to recover a pair of latent fingerprints from the weapon."

"Those guys are awesome."

"It gets better. The prints were identified as Trey Becker's."

"What?" Seth's jaw dropped. He twisted the wheel and whipped a quick U-turn. "Ted, I'll be right there."

NINE

Paige swept through the front door and stepped onto the porch. She hollered for Laser. She'd let him out thirty minutes earlier, and by now he'd usually be scratching to come in. She listened intently, then frowned. Where was that pup? She walked to the end of the porch and called again.

Leaves rustled, and wind sighed through the branches of the trees, nearly drowning out the sound of a distant yip and growl. *Laser.*

What was he up to? Probably chasing a squirrel or deer. Regardless, he was out of earshot and needed to get back to the house. Seth would never forgive her if something happened to his dog on her watch.

Stepping back inside, Paige popped her head in the kitchen to find Ruby putting away plates from the dishwasher. "I'll be right back. I'm going to check on Laser. He's not coming when I call."

Ruby eyed her. "That's fine, but remember he's partially deaf."

Selective hearing seemed a better description. Still, Paige wanted to make sure he hadn't gotten himself into trouble. She shrugged into her jacket, grabbed Laser's leash, stepped outside and closed the door. Cupping her hands around her mouth, she hollered one more time, "Laser."

She heard a faint bark and more growling coming from the right side of the house. Descending the steps, she zipped up her jacket and took off, following the sloping footpath she and Seth used to take to the small natural pond on the border of the lot.

Threading her way through the dense brush, the clean, fresh scents of pine and cedar lingering in the air awakened memories of better days. She used to love to walk these woods with Seth, talking and laughing, making plans for their future.

Before she could get all sentimental, another loud bark came from the direction of the pond. She refocused and picked up her pace. There were plenty of things Laser could get caught up in down there. She recalled fallen trees and old sections of barbed-wire fencing.

As she hurried the trail began to shrink around her, withering down to a thin, overgrown path. Huge trees towered on either side, keeping the pond well hidden.

When she hit an area of thornbushes and weeds, she left the path and tore through a thicket of brush, coming out into a muddy field. The picturesque pond appeared, and as she veered toward it, she noticed a truck parked in a dense area of forest.

Heart quaking, Paige left the small clearing and slipped into the trees. Terror snaked down her spine.

White, long bed, extended cab. The truck that ran her off the road.

Abandoned. At least for the moment.

But she had no delusions that whoever had parked it there had come looking for her. Looking to kill her.

Protective instincts screamed for Paige to run. To hide.

Save herself. But she ordered herself to stay calm. She needed to think. Not be impulsive. *Lord, help me.*

Finally her brain kicked into gear. She scanned the area, searching for anyone, any movement. Breathing with relief, she took note of the license tag.

But something rustled behind her, and she wheeled around, adrenaline surging, her mouth open, ready to scream…and then she saw Laser bound out of the trees.

A deep breath reset her heartbeat. Dropping into a crouch, she captured Laser in her arms. "Good boy. But no more barking, okay?" she whispered and fastened the leash to his collar, praying the guy wasn't within earshot.

She got to her feet. They needed to get out of there, before he came back. She grabbed her cell phone from her coat pocket and took off with Laser into the shelter of the trees. She didn't bother to call 911, not when Seth was the only person who knew this terrain.

Pick up. Pick up. There was no time to waste. The truck's owner could show back up any second. She fought against the stab of stark panic when her call went to voice mail again. "Seth, please get back to the cabin ASAP." Paige sputtered out details, the words coming a mile a minute.

Keeping a death grip on Laser's leash, she wrestled in a breath to fend off the panic as she tried to determine what to do next. *The highway.* It wasn't too far, and once they got there she could flag someone down. Terror climbed into her throat as she remembered Ruby was still at the cabin.

Fumbling with her cell phone, she stopped short, frantically punching in Seth's home number, grateful she still remembered it. Finally, it started to ring. But the call went straight to the answering machine. She left another message, this time a warning for Ruby.

"Come on, Laser." Heart pounding, she pulled on his leash and they both took off, running back in the direction of the cabin. She couldn't leave Ruby alone to fend off a murderer. *Lord, help me and keep Ruby safe*, she prayed as she frantically worked to dial 911. She pressed the phone to her ear. The deputies shouldn't have a problem finding the house. It started to ring. The call dropped.

No coverage.

No! Her mind screamed. Seth had always had spotty phone reception out here, the one thing she disliked about this place. Now more than ever.

At the end of the path, instead of going left toward the cabin, she kept straight, staying deep in the tree line, trying to keep out of sight, even though she'd have to walk twice as far to get to her destination.

The rustle of leaves, then the thud of booted footsteps hit her ears. She stopped, her breath coming in short spurts. Her eyes darted around her, and she caught a slight flicker of movement in a stand of bushy cedars. She gave Laser's leash a tug and guided him behind a large oak tree in an area of thick brush praying he wouldn't make a peep. Heart thudding, she peered through the dense forest. A man dressed in black and gray camo gear stood about fifty yards away near a pile of stacked logs. He shifted his feet, and that's when she saw the ski mask covering his face and the gun in his hand. Her heart stopped. He appeared to be watching the house. Ready to make his move.

She froze. Fear exploded in her chest. She was looking at her perpetrator. The man who wanted to kill her.

Panic crawled up her spine, and she knew she needed to get out of there. But something in the man's stance or the way he held the gun made her aware that it would only take one wrong move and she'd be dead.

A threatening growl escaped Laser's throat. *No!* Paige cringed. She crouched beside him, rubbed his head, trying to keep him quiet.

But it was too late.

The woods fell silent except for the crunch and snapping of twigs under the man's boots as he stalked toward her, his head moving vigilantly from side to side like a lion on a hunt for his prey.

A bleak and chilling terror settled over her. This was it.

He stopped and for a full minute stood just several yards away. Stock-still, chest heaving, still searching.

Her fingers fisted around the leash as Laser stayed at her side, lips raised in a snarl, ears pinned back. Her heartbeat pounded in her ears, a loud whooshing sound that broke up the tense silence.

Abruptly, the man turned, his solid footsteps moving in the opposite direction, away from her. Her heart danced. He was leaving, hopefully giving up and heading back to his truck.

Please, Lord. She breathed a sigh of relief, and at the same time Laser let loose another growl.

The man's retreating footsteps halted, and he swung back around. Before she could get to her feet and bolt out of there, he was standing just two feet away, his cold gray eyes glaring down at her. "Get up on your feet, Paige, and turn around." The creep had a husky, mumbled drawl, obviously trying to disguise his voice.

Not waiting for her to respond, he took a step and yanked her by the arm, jerking her to her feet. Paige sucked back a squeal as his grip bit into her arm. "I said on your feet. Now turn around." He shoved her, turning her away from him.

Her heart stalled in her chest. The man wanted to kill

her, and yet he was too much of a coward to show his face. Even with a mask on.

Laser jumped and growled in protest beside them. The man grabbed a fistful of her hair and forced her toward him. "Get the leash."

"It's okay, Laser." Paige reached for the leash and handed it to the man, praying he wouldn't hurt the dog.

Jerking her upright, the man slung the end around the branch of tree. As Laser strained the leash trying to break free, his barks and growls faded into the wind as the man's gravelly voice pulsed low in her ear. "You shouldn't have come back, Paige. Because of you a lot of people have had to suffer."

Amy came to mind, but she stayed mum, swallowing the lump of regret crowding her throat. She didn't want to give him one bit of acknowledgment for what he'd done.

"Do you know how much trouble you've caused?"

Paige bit her lip, tempering the urge to blurt out the truth—that he was the one who was wreaking havoc on the lives of so many.

"Let's go." He shoved her again. "We have a long walk ahead of us."

The words hit her like a sledgehammer. She tried to breathe, to keep her heart from beating out of her chest as a terrifying image whipped up in her mind. What did this maniac have planned for her?

Hysteria took over then, triggering fight-or-flight mode. By pure instinct, she took off in a sprint. She wasn't going anywhere with him voluntarily.

The man lunged after her, thudding her into the ground, knocking the air from her chest. A scream tangled in her lungs. She bucked and thrashed against him, terror twisting through her as she struggled to breathe.

Laser's barks and growls intensified, echoing around them.

"Stop while you're ahead, Paige." He clamped his beefy hand over her mouth, his garbled whisper hot and fast on her neck. "No one can hear you. No one can help you." His deep, exaggerated drawl made her skin crawl.

A scream scuttled up her throat, muffled by his harsh, callused hand. She fought harder. No way would she give in that easy. As the brute shifted a little, she was able to wrestle in a raspy breath. Adrenaline surged in her blood, and she slammed her elbow into his solar plexus.

The man's deep groan jarred in her eardrums. In her next heartbeat, she felt the cold metal barrel of his revolver pointed at her temple. She stopped moving. Tears welled. Her heart ached. A sob built in her chest.

She was going to die. Right here. Right now.

Laser thought differently. His surly snarl turned razor sharp, followed by the snap of the branch. Suddenly Laser was free and lunging at the man. *Thank you, Laser!* Paige wrestled out of her captor's grip as Laser took over, trying to maul him.

She couldn't stop the terror that darted through her as she took off at a run. What if the creep hurt Laser?

She shot up a quick prayer, begging for God's mercy and grace as she raced through the slick and rocky terrain, dodging low branches and skirting around boulders and trees. She couldn't bear it if one more life had to suffer on her behalf.

Laser's barks and growls rose above the rush of blood pounding in her eardrums and mingled with the man's violent yelling. "Get down, mutt! Get away!"

A single shot ripped through the air.

Paige stumbled, nearly losing her balance again as anguish slammed into her. *Please, Lord, not Laser! Please!*

"Paige, you'll be sorry for this!" The man's angry drawl rumbled in the distance.

Keep yelling! Tears scalded her eyes, blurring her vision. She stepped up her pace. Maybe the distant neighbors would hear him.

Two more rapid shots rang out and echoed around her.

Panic sprinted through her. She dashed through ten feet of clearing and dropped into the trees and even then didn't slow down.

More bullets hurtled through the air from behind, kicking up the dirt around her feet. Her shoes slipped on leaves still damp from the storm. She hit the ground hard, then scrambled back to her feet. Then she flew toward the underbrush as another bullet whizzed past her ear.

"Thanks, Ted, for keeping me updated." Seth handed Ted back the report. If finding Trey's fingerprints on the gun used in yesterday's parking-lot shooting didn't blow a hole in the case against Trey, he didn't know what would. The fact that Trey had been locked up for months for Madison's murder clawed at his gut. "I want Gentry picked up."

"And charge him with what?" A crease appeared between Ted's thick brows.

Good question. Seth thought on that for a moment, fighting the annoyance niggling his gut, telling him he was probably jumping the gun. Speculation and hearsay were never enough. They needed some sort of tangible evidence that would stick.

"I don't know." Seth ran his hand over his head. "I want Gentry off the streets, but for longer than a trip to the magistrate's office. Keep digging and I'll do the same. Hopefully we can come up with some noteworthy evidence that will keep him behind bars."

"I'll get right on it." Ted clapped his shoulder. "In the meantime, take care of Paige. I think our killer is getting desperate."

Desperate. Yes, the creep was desperate to kill Paige. Disgust seared Seth's gut at the reminder, making him even more amped up and ready to take Paige's attacker down. "Put a tail on Gentry." At least he could do that much.

"You've got it." Ted nodded.

Seth walked out of Ted's office feeling like he'd just been hit by a Mack truck. With Trey's trial in less than a week, Paige's perpetrator would be on the warpath, even more now than before. No matter where Paige was, in Boone or elsewhere, her life would be in danger. Seth had a feeling that what had started out as a situation derived from fear of being found out had morphed into a personal vendetta against Paige. Sociopaths didn't like to lose.

Seth stowed his jacket in the backseat of the truck and then climbed behind the wheel and started the engine. As he pulled out his phone, the blinking green light notified him of a missed call.

He punched the message button, and his heart shot into an unsteady rhythm as he listened to Paige. "Seth, you need to get back to the cabin ASAP. A white long-bed extended-cab truck is parked at the south end of the pond on your property…"

Her voice communicated everything he was feeling—terror, anger, disbelief.

The truck being there meant Paige's pursuer was somewhere in his woods. Even worse, the two women he loved most were danger. Panic rioted through him as he slammed the gearshift into Reverse and took off out of the employee lot.

Five seconds later he was on the highway heading north toward the cabin, his phone to his ear calling for backup. "I need every available officer on the property, now! Marked cars. Lights and sirens." He wanted the creep to know they were coming. A deterrent to hopefully foil his plans. "And put out an APB on a white long-bed Ford truck, extended cab." Just in case he was already gone.

He hoped he was. Prayed he was. Without leaving any casualties.

The road was clear, with no traffic in either direction. Seth increased his speed and squinted as the glare of the sun reflected off the windshield. Dialing Paige, he held his breath as he counted the number of rings. It went to six before her voice mail picked up. He swallowed back fear. "Hang in there, Paige. I'm on my way."

Guilt rode his shoulders. What if he was too late? The one day he'd silenced his phone... Teeth grinding, he shook his head. He'd made a point to have his phone on him at all times. He never missed a call or text.

Pressing his phone to his ear, he waited for his mom to pick up. His heart clenched and constricted harder with each unanswered ring. Finally, he heard her voice. "Hello."

"Mom, are you okay?" he asked, trying to keep the panic from his voice.

"Well, yes, dear, why wouldn't I be?"

Seth breathed a small relief. "How about Paige? Is she there with you?"

"No. She left a little while ago to look for Laser. And actually, I just let him back in. He came back yelping and has a slight limp. He must have gotten into something. I was just getting my shoes on to go look for her."

Seth's jaw clenched as he absorbed the news. Exactly the answer he didn't want to hear. Paige was out in the woods alone with *him*. Seth's fingers tightened into a death grip on the steering wheel as he steered the truck along the blind curve in the road. The ultimate nightmare had begun.

"No, Mom, don't go out after Paige. Just stay put where you are."

"Seth, you've got me worried now. Is everything okay?"

"Just keep the doors locked. Stay away from the windows. Get the hunting rifle out of my room and use it if you need to."

"Seth—"

He hit the disconnect key. There was no time to explain. He tried Paige again. Six more rings and the call went to voice mail. He didn't leave another message.

Slamming the phone back in his pocket, he sat up straighter, disappointment mounting. He found himself struggling to control his fear, lock it away. But the harder he tried, the worse it became. He took a steadying breath. *God, please protect her.*

Down the road and around the bend, he was about a half a mile away from his final turn when he saw the amber and red warning lights start to flash, heard a loud horn from the approaching northbound train, followed by the monotonous *ding-ding-ding* of the crossing bell.

Stomping on the brakes, Seth heaved a groan and slammed his fist against the steering wheel. *This can't be happening.*

Frantically, Paige pushed forward, belly crawling against loose dirt and rocks as she worked her way down a slight incline, keeping hidden by the tall grass and weeds, hopefully out of the line of fire.

Gunshots echoed. Feet pounded from behind. Using her elbows and toes, Paige forced herself to pick up speed, ignoring the bite of the rough terrain. Why hadn't she stayed in the cabin? Never let Laser out?

Laser. Her heart crimped, regret biting deep. Hopefully, he was okay.

When she came to the end of the tree line, Paige stumbled to her feet, weariness washing over her. The driveway lay just ahead of her, a few yards away. If she could just get to the end of it, maybe help would be coming by then.

Breathing hard, she forced herself to run, resisting the urge to look back. She couldn't stop now, even if escape seemed futile.

A bloodcurdling scream lit the air from behind her, followed by unintelligible words Paige couldn't make out. She ran harder, chest heaving, her rapidly pounding footsteps overshadowed by the sound of an approaching vehicle. *Yes, Lord!* The creep heard it, too.

The truck came screaming down the narrow drive, the vehicle's rear tires flinging gravel and dirt as it bounced over the rocks and ruts.

For a moment she couldn't make out the truck, but a split second later her heart rejoiced, relief flooding through her. It was Seth.

She would never discount his presence in her life again. He was her knight in shining armor.

Skidding to a stop on the side of the driveway, she placed a hand to her chest, trying to catch her breath. She was exhausted, throat parched, limbs weak.

A few feet away, Seth slammed to a stop and jumped out of his truck. "Are you okay?" He rushed to her. Suddenly she was in his arms, not even sure how she got there. Tears poured from her eyes as she buried her face in the soft fabric of his shirt. She closed her eyes as he held her. She'd never felt so safe or secure. A temporary rush of relief washed over her, blotting out the terror.

"Tell me what happened," he whispered against her hair.

Suddenly, Paige stiffened. Easing back, she raised her eyes to his, panic skittering up her spine. "He's here. The man—" She could barely get the words out as she pointed. "He was right behind me and has a gun. He's parked in the clearing near the pond."

"Who is he?"

"I don't know. He was wearing a ski mask."

Seth's face changed from concerned to enraged in a matter of moments. "Okay. Let's go." He grabbed her hand, and they took off for the truck.

Paige held on as Seth yanked the wheel to the left and the truck bounced off the driveway onto the side of the road. The four-wheel drive kicked in, and the wheels dug into the dirt and mud, churning over the rutted terrain.

"Turn left here," Paige shouted, pointing at a narrow dirt road. "That's the area where the truck was."

Seth took the turn, the road giving way to a footpath, and he slowed as the path grew thinner until it practically disappeared. Seth stopped and leaped out of the truck. Paige scurried out right behind him.

"Hold on. You better stay in the truck." Seth kept his voice low. "Stay down and keep the doors locked. Backup should be pulling up anytime. They have detailed directions on where the pond is."

Not on your life. Paige stepped away from the truck. "No, I'm going with you."

"Paige—never mind," Seth huffed, then beckoned her to him. "Just stay behind me."

They headed into the woods, Seth leading, gun drawn, his gaze constantly sweeping the area around them. Paige stayed close behind, heart thumping, praying for a positive outcome. As they drew closer, near the edge of the trees, sirens roared to life in the distance. Instant relief fluttered through her.

"The gang's all here," Seth whispered.

"Hopefully my attacker is still hanging around."

"We'll soon find out."

As they stepped out into the clearing, her heart dropped as she took in an unobstructed view of the pond. The truck was gone.

TEN

"Are you saying last week Gentry rented a truck that you believe was involved in Paige's accident?" Brett firmly positioned his hands on his hips, his face set in a fiery stare.

"That's correct." Seth leaned back in his seat at his dining room table, still not believing it himself. "We ran the plates from the truck Paige saw parked down by my pond earlier this afternoon. We found it to be a rental that Gentry picked up in Wilkes County the day Paige arrived in Boone. And although it was supposed to be returned within twenty-four hours, he held on to it, my guess is because of the damaged right door and fender from when he ran Paige off the road. So we can only assume it was Gentry that was out here today..." He gave Brett a short synopsis, bringing him up to speed on everything that had happened.

"I can't believe you're telling me this now—" Brett paused to look at his watch "—two hours after everything went down. I hate learning about critical information after the fact."

Seth had been a little preoccupied with Paige's safety. And trying to run down a killer. But apparently that wasn't a good enough reason for him not to pick up the phone in the heat of the action and fill Brett in on his next move. *Brother.* He hated this partner stuff. Seth shifted in his seat and expelled a breath through his nose, taking a moment to compose himself. Afraid he might say something he would regret.

"Sorry, I got busy," he finally said. Not a great excuse, but the best he had. "Nonetheless, we made progress today. So here's where we are now. The magistrate just issued warrants for Gentry's arrest and for a search of his home. I expect him to be brought in anytime now."

"Just great." Brett scowled, shaking his head. "Warrants are out and I was never even notified. I take one day off and my position on the case is totally disregarded—" His voice was a whine as he droned on. Seth tuned him out, focusing instead on Paige, who stepped into the room, her hair wrapped up in a towel, just out the shower. She looked refreshed. Happy. Like a thousand-pound weight had been lifted off her shoulders. Just her being there definitely softened the mood in the room.

And from seeing her this relaxed, Seth hadn't expected the gut-punch reaction reminding him how much he'd missed the old Paige.

Guilt nudged him from every direction as he thought about the stress that she'd been dealing with over the last ten months. Much to his chagrin, he'd contributed to that stress. Not because of Trey's arrest—there was only so much he could do with the evidence he had—but he'd let her walk away. He should have pushed his own fears aside and gone after her, been there for her. Not let her walk through this journey alone.

Twenty-twenty vision, too late.

To keep from giving in to a sigh, he cleared his throat, knowing at some point he needed to make amends with

Paige. He wanted her to know that he cared about what she'd been going through.

"Paige." The annoyance in Brett's voice cut through Seth's thoughts. "You do know to call me, even on my day off?"

The grimace pulling the edge of Brett's mouth told Seth that he wasn't going to let this go easily.

"Yes. Of course I knew that." A hint of confusion creased Paige's brow and settled into her eyes as she took the seat across from Seth. She unraveled the towel from her hair, draping it across the back of her chair. "I'm sorry, everything was happening so fast I guess I just didn't think about it." Combing her fingers through her damp hair, she sent Seth an uneasy look, as if she wasn't sure where this was going.

Seth knew exactly where this was headed, but before Brett succeeded with his attempt to provoke him into an argument, Seth was going to focus on something more positive. Like the strides they were making in their attempt to track down a killer.

Taking a deep breath, Seth pushed back in his chair. It had been a difficult enough day without having to placate Brett's sore ego. "Brett, it looks like we've got a good case against Gentry. Do you plan to talk to him once he's brought in? Or would you like me to?"

Brett jerked his head up, apparently caught off guard by the question. "Yes...of course I'll talk to him." The hard lines in his face softened a bit. "I doubt I'll get much, but I'll see what I can do."

Good. New focus. Seth got up to usher Brett out. "Sounds like a plan. Let me know how it goes."

"I will." Brett still had a hard tone, but it was less hostile now. He paced a few steps to the door, then stopped. "So Seth, what's your gut feeling in regard to Madison's murder? Do you believe Gentry's responsible for kill-ing his sister and framing Trey?" Brett's eyes probed Seth's face.

Seth shrugged and said, "I think the possibility is there. Trey's shotgun showing up tells us someone had ac-cess to his things before Madison's murder. Which could include the knife that killed Madison. And who better to have an extra key to his home than a family member?"

"It still seems like a long shot." Brett's voice went flat. "Unless you find some good evidence to support it."

"That's what we're working on." He clapped Brett on the shoulder. "Let me know what you come up with."

Seth closed and locked the front door behind Brett. As he turned around, Paige stood there, chin high, her expression nearly a smirk. "You never answered Brett's question."

Seth settled his hands on his hips, his eyes narrowed. "Which question was that?" He thought he'd addressed Brett's questions pretty thoroughly.

She shook her head, brows lifting to new heights. "He asked what your *gut* feeling was about Madison's mur-der. You just gave a vague answer. So, I'd like to know, do you really think my brother was involved?"

Seth wished his opinion wasn't so important to her. He'd let Paige down once by not coming to her rescue. Not being the support system she needed. The last thing he wanted was to give her false hope. Even if he be-lieved Trey was innocent—and he still wasn't completely convinced—everything remained up in the air, so he preferred to let that question ride.

"Seth? What do you think?" Her glittering green gaze locked on his.

But, of course, Paige thought differently. Seth bit back a sigh. "Paige, considering the recent developments, I think things are definitely looking more favorable for Trey."

"But what does your gut say?" she asked him point-blank, not blinking an eyelash. "You always advised me to trust my gut instinct, so I'd like to know if your instinct has changed about my brother."

Seth wasn't even sure he'd had a gut instinct after Trey's arrest. In fact there had been nothing personal in his decision to name Trey the prime suspect in his wife's murder. Seth was bound by the evidence that had been collected, something Paige still failed to understand. And now, even with new evidence, his gut was still waffling on who'd killed Madison.

Paige tilted her head, her gaze not leaving his face.

She wanted his complete allegiance to her brother. Which he couldn't give her at the moment. One more thing to keep their relationship strained. He cleared his voice. "Well, like I said, I definitely have a better feeling about Trey—"

A thunderous crash came from across the room. Paige's squeal lit the air as she sprang forward into his arms. "What was that!"

Instinctively, his arms came around her, and he pulled her into his embrace.

A yip and a bark followed.

Seth snickered as he shot a quick glance down the hall to the dining room, where a bundle of wood trim normally stacked against the wall was scattered across the floor. Beside it, Laser panted and sniffed as he went about trying to investigate. "Laser, buddy, you need to watch where you're going."

Of course, it didn't help that they were living in a construction zone.

"Is he okay?" Paige asked, still hovering in his embrace. He felt the slight tremor pass through her body as her arms around his waist tightened and her heart beat rapidly in sync with his own. She was scared, even if she worked hard to conceal it.

"Laser's fine. He must be in a curious mood. That wood hasn't budged since I piled it there months ago," Seth said, tightening his hold around her, bracing himself for the irrational pang in his chest that always followed whenever he allowed his guard to slip around Paige. Quite aware that he was treading back on dangerous ground.

"Well, his curiosity paid off. As did his protective nature. He really came to my rescue today."

Seth was grateful for his old hound. "Laser's got a good nose for trouble." And he was equally attuned to good character. He'd loved Paige the moment he met her and still did. Loyal to the end.

Oddly, Seth's heart skidded to a halt at that knowledge. Better than the loyalty he'd displayed. He'd left Paige hanging when she needed him. He should have come to her rescue. Supported her, paid more attention to her gut instincts earlier. A woman like Paige, with all her goodness and faith, deserved better than that. And as much as he still cared for her, she deserved someone better than him. The battle within him at that thought nearly had him pulling back and releasing his protective hold on her.

But for the moment, he'd endure. This wasn't about him. And Paige needed comfort.

"What was that horrific noise?" his mother called from the top of the stairs.

Immediately, Paige jerked away, and with great reluctance, Seth released her, a sudden coolness taking her place. She stared up the staircase at Ruby, a deep flush on her cheeks. "Oh, that was just Laser. He knocked over some wood."

Obviously, she was embarrassed about being caught in his arms. Which only reaffirmed what he already knew—Paige had moved on. And he didn't blame her.

Later that evening Paige peered out the window of the guest bedroom, still trying to process everything that had unfolded that day. Gentry was now the prime suspect in the attacks against her and was also being investigated in Amy's and Madison's murders.

Emotion welled up in her chest. After all the worries, all her scheming to find out the truth of Madison's murder, they were finally onto something. *Thank You, Lord.*

She took a deep, fortifying breath.

Her brother wasn't off the hook yet, but she had this gut feeling that his case was ready to crack wide-open. And with that belief, contentedness filled her soul.

Ten long months, and soon this nightmare would be over. Her brother would finally be free, finally walking out of jail, moving forward in his life. She couldn't be happier for him.

But what about her? Where would she be?

Once Trey was released, she wouldn't have anything tying her to Durham. It was a pleasant town, but not where she'd hoped to build her future. Although nowhere in particular came to mind when she thought about where she would like to settle down.

She and Trey had moved around a lot when they were growing up. It wasn't until she followed Trey to Boone after his stint in the military that she finally felt she'd found a home. A place where she could settle down. Fall in love. Get married. Raise a family.

But that short-lived dream died with Trey's arrest.

Her picture-perfect world shattered by deception and heartbreak.

A fist of grief squeezed her heart. For the first time since her brother's arrest, her frustration and anger subsided enough for her to see more clearly how things had transpired. All this time she'd held a grudge against Seth for her feeling of abandonment.

Feelings don't always equal reality. Paige often spoke that truth to the patients she counseled, but she now saw how true it was in her own life. Despite all the drama involving her brother, she now blamed herself for walking—no, running—away from the man she loved. She'd been so caught up in her brother's troubles she might have expected more than was reasonable from Seth.

Paige eased down on the edge of the bed and folded her arms. Seth wasn't the one who had changed—it was her. He'd always poured both his heart and soul into his job and never compromised what he thought was right, even when it meant locking her brother behind bars.

Now, looking back, she knew she could have been more understanding of his plight, but at the time she didn't have the mental capacity to fight for her brother's release and support Seth in his decision that her brother was guilty.

Paige ground her teeth in quiet frustration. She rested her arm against the windowsill, trying to rein in her whirling thoughts. A sob rolled up her throat.

She couldn't change the past, and the reality was Seth was no longer part of her future.

But that's okay. Paige adjusted her attitude, suddenly annoyed with herself. It was all worth it. Every minute. Every prayer. Every sacrifice she made. If that's what it took to get her brother released.

She swiped her hands at her eyes, brushing away the tears that stung them. Trey gaining his freedom was all that mattered. Wherever she ended up, she'd get along just fine. And with God leading the way, she had nothing to fear. In fact, she looked forward to whatever new adventure was in store for her.

She felt a calming of her spirit in that.

Quietly, she listened to the wind rustling the leaves left on the trees. She turned back to the window and peered out. The yellow moon hung high in a black sky. A sliver of gold against a twinkling backdrop of stars.

So different than the day she arrived back in Boone. A raging storm, no moon or a star in the sky and a killer on her tail. Not the welcome she had hoped for, but worth it all the same.

She climbed under the covers and turned off the light, confident that in a few days this would all be behind her.

Trey would be free and everything in her life would be fine.

Well, almost.

The next morning, Paige was up bright and early. Feeling refreshed, she got dressed, and by the time she went downstairs, Seth was already sitting at the table with his cell phone to his ear.

Paige accepted a cup of tea from Ruby and settled in the chair across from Seth.

"Okay, Ted, thanks." Seth hung up, snickering softly. He raised an eyebrow at her. "I think we just hit pay dirt."

Seth's statement brought Paige straight up in her seat. She set her cup on the table, her hands shaking. "You found something conclusive that would help my brother?"

Seth leaned forward with a satisfied grin. "A small arsenal of weapons was seized during the search of Gentry's house. Rifles, handguns, along with some military knives and various firearm magazines and ammunition. And of the firearms confiscated, one was a commemorative pistol with Trey's initials on it."

"Which means…"

"Which means Gentry had access to Trey's weapons, which would make setting him up for Madison's murder a viable possibility. Gentry's financial issues only add to the suspicion."

"This is crazy… I mean, incredible." Paige rubbed at her forehead, trying to take it all in. "I remember Trey mentioning that Madison's mother had a key to their home while they were married. So, I guess Gentry having access to Trey's weapons wouldn't have been difficult."

"Do you recall if Trey changed the locks when Madison moved out?"

Paige shook her head. "I doubt it. He had no reason to lock Madison out. He wanted her back."

"That's what I figured." Seth leaned back in his seat. "I had the information sent to Trey's attorney. Although there will still be an investigation into the murder, Trey's trial will be postponed due to the new evidence. And since he is no longer the only suspect, bail will be set for his release."

A sense of elation blended with relief. "So when will my brother be released?" she asked, tears of joy choking her voice.

"If his attorney does his job right, it could be as early as tomorrow."

Her heart danced in her chest. That gave her plenty of time to get her things together and get back to Durham. She wanted to be there to greet Trey when he walked out of that horrible place.

"Breakfast, anyone?" Ruby walked into the room carrying a tray bearing jam, napkins and a plate of biscuits. She set it on the table. "There's still hot water if either of you would like more tea."

"Oh, no thank you, Ruby," Paige said, breathing deep, trying to reset the jitterbug rhythm in her chest. The excitement exploding inside her was hard to curtail.

"I'm good, too, Mom," Seth said, grabbing a biscuit.

"So, Paige." Ruby slipped into the seat beside her. "Now that your safety concerns have subsided and Trey's situation is looking better, what are your plans?" At the hopeful gleam in Ruby's eye, the excitement inside Paige started to dissipate. A sore subject, and Paige knew why Ruby was asking.

"All I have planned for the time being is to head back to Durham," Paige said, shifting in her seat as renewed tension crept back along her nerve endings. "But as things calm down more with Trey, I'd love to catch up with you and see what you've done with the house." Paige took a sip of her tea, trying to play it cool.

Ignoring her attempt at a shift in conversation, Ruby turned in her chair to eye Paige more closely. "No plans to come back to Boone?"

Paige swallowed the hot liquid a little too quickly. She cleared her throat to keep from choking. "Not at the moment, no." Or ever, but she wasn't about to go there. She knew what Ruby was hinting at. She wanted nothing more than for Paige and Seth to get back together. Get married and supply her with a quiver of grandchildren.

"Well, I hope you'll decide to come back. I know Seth would like that, too."

Paige slowly sank down in her chair when she heard Seth choke. He took a drink. Cleared his throat. If she'd had any doubt as to Seth's thoughts about her, she knew now that even as he attempted to keep her safe, he had no other feelings in regard to romance. None whatsoever.

Which was just fine. As it should be. Paige firmly reiterated that to herself even as her heart slipped to her knees.

A half hour later, she was packed and ready to leave. She parked her rolling suitcase by the front door, leaving her computer bag and purse beside it.

Her eyes flicked to the clock on the entry wall. Ten after nine. Time to get going.

Seth had agreed to drop her off at Tessa's condo. She had a few loose ends to tie up in town, and then she'd be off to Durham tomorrow.

To see her brother walk out of jail.

Her heart swelled with gratitude as she thought about the new evidence. Finally, something would shed doubt on her brother's guilt. She thought about Trey and the jaw-splitting grin on his face when he heard the news. And she couldn't wait to wrap him in a hug, the first one in ten months.

Even as tears of joy moistened her eyes, a deep sadness enveloped her when she thought about how her life was about to change. Tomorrow she'd head out of town for the last time. She had to admit she'd miss some things here. The beautiful sunsets. Spring flowers. Long walks through the woods. Working on the cabin with Seth. The sound of his laughter. His sweet kisses…

Swallowing a sigh, Paige gave herself a mental shake. This emotional seesaw she was on had to stop right now. She'd accomplished what she set out to do and she needed to keep it together. No regrets. Focus on the future. Hers and Trey's.

Feeling better, Paige shook off her grief and walked purposefully toward the kitchen. Standing in the doorway, she eyed Seth, his back to her as he poured himself another cup of tea. Ruby stood beside him, busy at the sink.

Paige hesitated, her eyes straying from one side of the room to the other, taking in the beauty of the kitchen. Rich walnut cabinets, granite countertops, warm hardwoods. The dream kitchen she'd always wanted. But it wasn't meant to be hers. She swallowed. "Seth, I'm ready whenever you are."

Ruby turned. "You're not leaving already?"

"Yes. I have to go." Paige forced a small smile. "I have a few things to do before I leave for Durham in the morning."

Tossing the dish towel on the counter, Ruby stepped toward her. "Paige, it was so good to see you. Please keep in touch."

Paige couldn't promise that, honestly. She fought her tears, hugging Ruby. "Thank you for everything."

Paige pulled away and saw Seth, standing off to the side, watching the interaction. The expression on his face was confusingly solemn. Was he deep in thought or maybe just ready to get her out of his hair? Or maybe, like her, just trying to keep his emotions in check.

Wishful thinking. No, delusional. She bit her bottom lip. The cold, harsh reality was she'd accomplished what she came to do and now it was time to leave. Alone.

Seth carried Paige's bags into Tessa's condo. As Paige walked with him to the door, sadness washed over him like an icy rain. Saying goodbye was never easy, even when he knew it was the best thing.

"Paige, I wish you all the happiness in the world," Seth said, pausing in the doorway. "And I'm glad things are working out in Trey's favor."

"Thank you for everything." Her smile held a hint of wistfulness, almost as though she wished things were different. Regret? Grief? Or maybe total exhaustion for all she'd been through. He'd never been good at reading her emotions or he would have done a better job of offering her support after Trey's arrest. A situation that he'd originally thought would die down eventually and Paige would understand that he was only doing his job by arresting Trey, but instead their relationship died altogether.

"Paige, take care of yourself. And remember, safety first. Always keep an eye on your surroundings and keep your cell phone close."

"As always, good advice, Detective." Paige rolled her lip in, fighting a smile. "Although I hope not to have a stalker to worry about again."

He hoped the same thing. "But..." He took a step closer, brushed a fallen lock of hair from her cheek. "It never hurts to play it safe and stay away from danger."

Her lips parted, and her eyes went wide. "And I plan to do that."

"Very wise decision." He smiled. "Because I would hate for anything to ever happen to you."

She looked up at him with eyes that shimmered with emotion. "I did have a few close calls, didn't I? And who would have believed Gentry was behind it? Some people just continue to amaze me."

"Gentry is only a suspect at the moment. Charged, but not convicted." Seth lifted a teasing brow, making a subtle point. He wanted her to understand how easy it was to make assumptions.

"Oh, my, you're correct," Paige blurted, a rush of pink staining her cheeks. Her gaze fastened on his, and he saw her bottom lip quiver. "I'm sorry, Seth. I wasn't the least bit understanding about the job you had to do."

Bitter regret smacked him in the chest, and he inhaled deeply to fill his lungs. And he hadn't tried hard enough to understand what she was going through. "Paige, I should have been there for you—"

"Seth, please. No regrets." Paige put a hand on his sleeve. "Let's just chalk it up as a tough emotional time for both of us."

Still, he had no excuse—he should have been there for her. But he wouldn't argue the point. Revisiting the pain and frustration didn't seem very productive.

"All right." He masked his discomfort with a forced grin.

"So I guess this is it?" Emotion gleamed in her eyes. "Tomorrow I'm out of here. And life gets back to normal for you."

Normal? He wasn't even sure normal existed for him anymore. A lump of emotion lodged in his throat. He realized now, too late, that he'd let the best thing in his life get away, and he accepted full responsibility.

As he swallowed, he was tempted to let go of common sense, of their past, the pain and the heartache and take her in his arms, hold her tight and never let her go.

Not a good idea, he reminded himself. And he would have walked away, if the unexpected longing rising inside him hadn't been stronger and more passionate than the feelings of remorse and sadness.

Taking a step closer, Seth slid his thumb over her soft cheek. "Here's to you, Paige, and your new endeavors." His voice rasped, showing his uncertainty of how Paige would react.

Instead of pulling away, Paige softened her gaze beneath his touch and leaned in. He caught the scent of her perfume. Sweet. Clean. Familiar.

His pulse raced, and before he could stop himself, he

slipped his arm around her waist. Pulling her close, he lowered his head; his lips captured hers. Softly. Tenderly. A perfect moment until…

The bleat of his cell phone slashed the air.

Paige stilled as if reality rang. She stepped back from his embrace, cold air filling the space where she'd just been. And from the look of misgiving on her face he knew he'd overstepped a boundary they'd set. His heart dropped. What was he thinking? He dug his cell from his pocket, chastising himself for not keeping a rein on his emotions.

He slammed his phone to his ear. "Garrison here."

"Morning, Seth."

"Hey, Ted, what's up?" Seth glanced at Paige, who was now inside the condo, busying herself with something in the kitchen.

"Gentry wants to meet with you."

Gentry? Seth sighed and tried to swallow back his frustration. He'd had enough of this guy. "Brett's already talked to him."

"He asked to talk to you specifically. No attorneys."

"Is he aware of his rights, that anything he says can be used against him?"

"Yep."

Seth rubbed his head, eyeing Paige now in the living room straightening up. He wanted to talk to her about what just happened, but… "I'll be right there." He'd already overstayed his welcome.

ELEVEN

Paige carried her last suitcase to her car, then hugged her friend goodbye. "Tessa, thanks for the use of your condo."

"No problem." Tessa perched a hip against the car fender and crossed her arms over her chest. "I'm just glad you're okay. I can't believe the week you had."

"It has been a long one, to say the least." Paige sighed deeply. "I appreciate you staying up with me last night, listening to me vent." She hadn't planned on unloading on Tessa, but one question led to another, and soon the whole chilling story was out. Speaking the timeline of events out loud unnerved her more than she thought, and she barely got a wink of sleep.

Tessa laughed. "Are you kidding? I should thank you. It was better than watching a suspense thriller."

Paige never liked thriller flicks. *Murder. Suspense. Running from a killer.* Fighting off a shiver, she cocked an eyebrow at her friend. "Hearing about it is definitely more entertaining than living through it."

"I'm sure you're right about that," Tessa agreed, brushing back strands of curly red hair. "But I do recall a few interesting moments. So, tell me more about Seth."

Seth. Paige fought not to wince. There wasn't much to say. He'd stepped up to keep her safe and now his job was done. She didn't wish to analyze the kiss too deeply. Emotions were running high for both of them. And when Seth came to his senses, he'd hightailed it out of there with barely a goodbye.

She half expected him to at least call and wish her well. But apparently he was having a busy morning. Paige checked her watch, saw it was past ten. "Oh, no, I need to go."

"Paige, you're not getting off the hook that easy."

"No, really." Paige looked at Tessa. "I made plans to stop and see Mrs. Cramer before I leave."

"Wait a minute," Tessa said, a look of confusion tugging her features. "Are you talking about *the* Mrs. Cramer, as in Gentry and Madison Cramer's mother?"

Paige nodded, not a hundred percent comfortable with the idea. "I got a call early this morning from one of the Cramers' employees. He told me how distraught she was over all that has happened. She just got into town last night and asked to see me. She really is a sweet woman. And she's lost so much."

"Sounds awkward." Tessa shook her head, then shrugged. "But if you're okay with it…"

She wasn't necessarily okay with it, but it was something she needed to do. The woman was suffering. She probably felt judged for what her son was charged with. Paige knew that feeling and how lonely it was. Yes, she needed to go. For Mrs. Cramer's sake and her own.

Paige pulled onto East King Street and headed out of town. She felt no regrets. She was staying positive, refusing to dwell on the missteps of her past. And now without the urgency of Trey's trial consuming her thoughts, she was ready to conquer the world of opportunities out there.

So why did she feel like her heart was breaking?

She gritted her teeth, forcing those thoughts away. Once she was out of Boone, she'd be fine.

She turned onto Clover Bend in the Willoughby Hills neighborhood where Mrs. Cramer lived. The road was long and winding and the houses too distant for her to feel completely at ease with stopping by. Maybe she should have arranged for a more neutral meeting place. Somewhere she could bug out if the conversation got awkward.

But she was already here and wouldn't stay long. Twenty minutes max and then she'd be on her way to Durham. And once she got there, she'd be off to the jail to pick up her brother.

Her heart fluttered with relief. She couldn't wait.

Paige got out of the car and stepped up to the porch. As she reached to ring the bell, she saw it was taped over with a note that read, "Paige, no need to knock. Please come in."

She felt somewhat better. She twisted the knob on the heavy wood door, walked inside and slid her sunglasses up to rest on her head. Once again apprehension skittered through her, along with a sudden chill that had nothing to do with the cool breeze whistling outside.

She saw no one. Heard nothing. If she was expected, wouldn't Mrs. Cramer make herself known?

Taking a couple steps, Paige panned her gaze around the living room. "Mrs. Cramer? It's Paige Becker."

"Paige, I'm so glad you're here."

Paige jumped, startled by the strong, masculine voice.

"Who are you?" Paige's voice faltered as she retreated a step. "Where are you?"

"Over here." The man's voice, deep and louder now, coming from the left, reached Paige's ear.

Paige turned to see Eli walking down a short hall toward her, a broad, crooked smile on his face. She gave a sigh of relief, once again chastising herself for being so jumpy.

"Oh, Eli, I'm glad you're here. Thanks for contacting me this morning. Is Mrs. Cramer still expecting me?"

"Yes. Let me take you to her office."

Paige crossed the foyer and followed Eli through the living room and then to a small office. He held open the door and ushered her in. "Have a seat while we wait for Mrs. Cramer."

"I don't have much time," Paige started to explain, taking the closest seat to the door. "I really need to get on the road."

"I understand." Eli draped his wide body along the edge of the desk, his expression calm, surprisingly friendly. "So, Paige, tell me something. Did you accomplish everything you came to town for?"

The question threw her into a momentary tailspin. What was he getting at? Paige cocked her head. "Sorry, Eli, I'm not sure what you're asking."

Palms up, he swept his hands wide. "You came back to Boone looking for something. Did you find it?" His clarification still gave her no inclination at where this was going.

"I came back to find information to help my brother." Paige swallowed, her throat dry, burning. Was this Eli's attempt at small talk, or was he trying to chastise her for Gentry's arrest? Either way she didn't feel comfortable talking about this. Paige cleared her throat. "Do you think Mrs. Cramer will join us soon? Because I really do need to get going."

"You didn't answer my question, Paige. Did you find what you came for?" He had a cold glint in his eyes, an edge of superiority in the set of his shoulders.

Gooseflesh pebbled her skin, and the reality of the situation hit home. Mrs. Cramer hadn't asked her to come—Eli had wanted her there.

To taunt her or...kill her?

The thought of either shot the acrid taste of bile up the back of her throat. "I'm sorry, but I really need to go." Paige heard her voice crack. She surged out of her seat and headed for the door. "Please give Mrs. Cramer my best."

Eli blocked the doorway. "It's not time for you to leave yet. Take a seat, please. I have something for you."

Paige froze, breath trapped in her throat. "No, I prefer to stand. Actually, I prefer to leave."

"Those are not options. Now, sit." Eli's shrewd gray eyes pierced all the way through to Paige's soul.

Paige started to back up, heart thudding. Her panic increased when Eli plunged his hand deep in his pocket.

She bumped into the chair before dropping back into it. With prayers flying, her eyes stayed glued on him. And she blinked in disbelief when instead of a gun, he pulled out a phone. *Her cell phone.* The one she lost the day she was run off the mountain.

She gaped, her insides churning, bile clawing its way up her throat. "It was you...not Gentry."

"Now, Paige, you have the information you came for. But unfortunately, it's knowledge you'll no longer need."

Seth shifted on his feet as he addressed the team of detectives in the conference room at the sheriff's department. "Gentry was pretty much having a meltdown." Seth summarized his meeting with Gentry from the day before. "He did admit to financial issues, stating he'd used up most of his mother's money along with his own. And of course he denies all allegations of murder and attacks on Paige's life, claiming instead that he'd been set up."

"That seems to be the name of the game for this investigation." Detective Colton Walsh's comment hit on a common thread in the room as chatter and comments picked up among the detectives.

"So what happened to his cocky, *you can't touch me* attitude?" Ted tipped back in his chair and eyed Seth directly.

"Gone," Seth said, shrugging. "He's scared."

"What about the white Ford pickup he rented? What's his explanation for that?" Chief Mullins asked from his seat between Ted and Colton.

"His company has an account with the rental car agency. They use them periodically and keep a credit card on file. Various employees pick up for the company, and he's insistent he hasn't been there in months."

Ted leaned forward in his seat, eyes wide as if a lightbulb just went off in his head. "Whose driver's license was on file?"

Excellent question. Seth had the same. "Ironically, the rental company couldn't find one. And the clerk that processed the rental agreement couldn't recall who picked up the vehicle. And as we all know, the truck is still missing and at this point considered stolen."

The chatter picked up again, the detective team airing their frustration. Except Brett, who stood at the back, arms folded, staring Seth down with granite eyes.

"Brett, is there anything you'd like to add?"

"No," Brett said, breathing hard through his nose. "You pretty much summed up everything Gentry told me when we first brought him in."

Good. They were on the same page, at least as far as Gentry.

"I'm just not sure why he requested to talk to you," Brett said, not breaking his stare.

Seth's jaw tensed at the question, and he had to stop himself from asking why it really mattered. Gentry had probably thought getting Seth on his side would be beneficial since he and Paige had dated. Or maybe he just didn't like Brett.

"So where does this all leave us?" the chief interjected, pushing up from his chair. "Because if we aren't a hundred percent sure Gentry is our man, we better get out there and find who is. I don't want to jeopardize another life in this town."

Seth nodded. "Agreed." And no, he wasn't a hundred percent confident about any part of the investigation. If they suspected someone had set Trey up, then why wouldn't it be plausible that Gentry had been also? Not saying he had that hunch, but until there was more credible evidence to tie to Gentry, he wasn't slamming the lid on the investigation. He was glad Paige was heading back to Durham. At least he wouldn't be worrying about the possibility of her getting more in harm's way. "The case is still active and will continue to be."

"Good. Keep me posted," the chief said as he walked out of the conference room.

The small team of detectives started to disperse.

"What do you think?" Ted asked Seth on his way out the door.

"I think we need more conclusive evidence. What we have now won't keep Gentry behind bars long."

"I'm sure his attorney is already scrambling."

"Yeah, I spoke to his mother this morning before I came in. She has some big-name criminal attorney coming in from Charlotte."

"Then we better get cracking." Ted paused before he turned toward his office. "By the way, how's Paige?"

Seth's heart stung at the question, but he didn't let it

show on his face. "She left today for Durham. Since we have another suspect, Trey will be assigned bail."

"Well, one less worry, not having Paige around."

"Yep" was all he said, then he headed down the hallway toward the exit.

In the parking lot he climbed into his truck and took off toward Gentry's home. It was now a crime scene due to the weapons found there, and he wanted to take a look around himself.

He glanced at the clock on the dash—10:50 a.m. Blowing a breath through clenched teeth, he gripped the steering wheel tighter. This day was already dragging. He had the same dank feeling as when Paige left the first time. Minutes felt like hours. Hours like days. It was slow going for a while, getting used to not having her around, but thankfully he'd eventually come to the conclusion that being apart was best for both of them.

Seth rolled his shoulders to stretch out a knot of tension, and as he thought about it, he realized he'd really never told her goodbye yesterday. He pulled out his phone, and before he could stop himself he dialed Paige's number.

The call went to voice mail.

Seth disconnected, unease knotting his gut.

There were a thousand reasons why she wouldn't pick up. Not wanting to talk to him not being the least of them. Still he'd rather know she was okay.

He clicked on his phone and asked Siri to find Tessa Riley's phone number.

Tessa picked up on the second ring. After they exchanged cordial greetings, he asked what time Paige had left.

"It hasn't been long, maybe forty-five minutes."

Paige was out of the county and well on her way. "I'm glad she got an early start."

"Actually, she planned to stop by and see Mrs. Cramer on her way out of town."

Mrs. Cramer? Confusion tumbled with dread. Seth pressed the phone harder against his ear. "What do you mean, she stopped by to see Mrs. Cramer? She isn't in town."

Tessa was quiet a moment. "Are you sure? Because according to Paige, she's back and asked to see her."

Seth had just spoken to the woman. She was in Charlotte. Two hours away. "Who gave Paige that information?"

"One of the Cramers' employees called Paige this morning. Do you think she's okay?" Tessa's voice was laced with panic.

"I'm heading there now to find out."

Heart thumping and with prayers flying, Seth swung his truck around and headed in the direction of Gentry's mother's house. He punched in Paige's number. *Answer, Paige. Please.* It went to voice mail again instead.

Dread filled his chest, and he stomped on the gas.

"Let it ring."

The harsh tenor of Eli's voice sent a shot of adrenaline through Paige's veins as she clutched her purse, absorbing each impatient blaring vibration.

"What do you want from me?" She swallowed, hearing the fear in her own words.

"I want this whole charade to end." He shoved her old cell phone in front of her eyes. Paige recoiled against the seat cushion, chastising herself for even coming today.

"I saw everything, Paige," Eli started his loud rant. "Your list of Madison's friends and colleagues. Phone numbers. Notes. You thought you were so smart, but both you and your *know-it-all* boyfriend still don't have a clue. Why couldn't you just leave things alone?" The more he rambled, the more panic squeezed her chest, her lungs nearly collapsing when he hurled the phone with hurricane force toward the wall, embedding it into the drywall.

"Do you understand how much trouble you've caused?"

Struggling for a deep breath, Paige straightened at his skewed comment. A déjà vu question from her attack in the woods. She'd caused trouble? "I just came back to help my brother." Her voice was a croak.

"And because of that more have suffered. Gentry's in jail. Amy's dead." His voice was more agitated now.

No, because of you, Eli, she wanted to scream. But she held on to to her composure and desperately tried to recall everything she knew about psychopathic killers. Careful planners. Proud of their work. Did all his victims have to hear him rant before they died?

She swallowed. She needed to keep him talking, maybe throw him off his agenda. Maybe she could distract him, change his mind.

The incensed look in his eyes told her otherwise.

Her heart dipped into her chest. *Lord, get me out of this mess.*

Because Seth, Brett—no one knew she was in danger.

She fought off the sting of tears. Eli was crazy, but she wouldn't give in to him. He'd already turned her life and her brother's upside down, and for what? That question burned deep and anger resurged. What kind of motivation drove someone like this?

Her head jerked high, and she sucked in a bolstering breath. "You set my brother up for Madison's murder. Why?"

Eli's tightened jaw signaled his dislike of the question. "Madison could never get that *no-good fool* brother of yours out of her head. I talked to her. Gentry talked to her. But she still wanted to go back to him."

Paige's mind was scrambling to catch up. Madison had still loved Trey. But who had killed her, Gentry or Eli?

"But selfishness is what did her in." His voice was a rasp. "A trait that you and she share."

What? "I—I don't understand."

Terror clutched at her throat as he hunkered down and got in her face. "Devoted to your own ruthless desires. Do you understand now?"

Paige backed away, gluing her head to the back of the chair. Was he insinuating that she was selfish for wanting to help her brother? This man was deranged.

But what about Madison? She didn't dare ask.

Without warning Eli sprang to his feet. He whirled around to the desk, and Paige's stomach bottomed out when she saw him yank the bottom drawer open and pull something out.

She needed to get out of there.

Pulse pumping, Paige took a quick inventory of the room. Three high windows, no outside doors, leaving her with one choice—her only way out was the way she'd come in.

When Eli turned, her pulse ratcheted higher at the sight of gloves and duct tape in his hands.

Acting purely on instinct, Paige shoved her purse under her arm and lunged for the doorway.

"Don't even consider it," Eli's voice roared from behind her.

But too late, Paige stumbled into the living room, her gaze darting to the large door in the foyer and then back to the French doors half the distance away.

She dashed twenty feet to the double glass doors, her heart banging against her ribs at the sound of footfalls pounding behind her. Grinding to a stop, she yanked on the knob, frantically trying to get out.

Nothing.

The door had a keyed dead bolt.

"No, you don't!" Eli's huge groping hands snatched at her.

Struggling wildly, Paige twisted and whirled out of his grasp. Her purse flung from her shoulder and the contents inside spewed across the floor with projectile force. Propelling herself forward, she swung toward the front of the house, praying somehow that door wasn't locked by the same type of dead bolt as the other.

"Why are you making this so difficult?" Eli's loud voice boomed through the house.

Was he kidding? Paige grabbed a lamp off the foyer table, her breath coming in short spurts. Hefting it over her head, she it hurled it like a grenade. Glass splintered and shattered as it crashed on the floor.

She saw fire blaze in Eli's eyes as he skidded to a stop.

Spinning on her heel, she ran to the front door and yanked on the knob. The door flew open, and she bolted outside. Fresh cool air hit her face, and as she scrambled for the porch steps, she felt strong, sweaty fingers latch on to her arm.

A scream hurled up her throat, cut short by the slap of Eli's gloved hand over her mouth.

"This was not part of the plan, Paige." He growled as he hauled her inside, her heels scraping across the wooden porch floor.

As Paige twisted and thrashed harder, he tightened his grip, her lungs locking as he swung around and bolted the door.

Her hopes crashed.

He was out of breath, and she struggled for air. "Now it's time you listen to me." His voice hitched, but his tone was even more forceful.

Then he gave a small, mirthless laugh. "You are like Madison. Stubborn. Selfish. A fighter to the end. She could have had everything if she had listened to me. Gentry was losing the business, we could have taken it from him, but no—" he grunted, his grip compressing her more "—she only wanted your brother."

Paige gasped as the room started to spin. Nausea rose, her extremities went numb.

"But we don't always get what we want, do we, Paige?"

Fueled by a potent mix of disgust and willpower, Paige mustered every ounce of strength and managed to buck against him.

"Stop it, now!" he screamed, his viselike grip loosening, enabled Paige to gulp air and thrash harder. "I said, stop!" He yanked her hard against him, one arm circling her neck to choke her as he pulled a gun.

Panic exploded in her chest. The fight was over.

Seth took off like a bullet over the tracks, traveling down the roadway toward Carol Ann Cramer's house. He'd called for backup, and as he tried Paige again, anger erupted in his gut when his call went to voice mail. If Paige was in any way hurt, whoever was involved better be ready to answer to him.

Seth swallowed the bile that surged up his throat. *Focus.* He didn't have time for distraction, something that would lead to disaster.

Gritting his teeth, Seth blew through a flashing yellow light and continued up the road. Only a couple more miles.

Thoughts and scenarios tangled in his head, and he nearly missed his turn. The truck fishtailed as Seth spun the wheel, careening haphazardly onto the road. Then, shifting gears, he punched the gas and sped down the bone-jarring, winding path.

Finally Mrs. Cramer's house came into view. Seth's heart surged into his throat when he spotted Paige's car parked out front. *God, please let her be okay.*

Seth slammed on his brakes; the truck came to a lurching stop. He jumped out, a cloud of dust and burning rubber filling his lungs.

Coughing to clear them, Seth flew up the walk to the front porch. Without hesitation, he gave three sharp raps on the door.

No answer.

Heart shattering inside his chest, he took a quick assessment of the door, knowing if he needed to he could take it down.

"Don't move or say a word," Eli whispered, jamming the gun into her spine.

Paige stood stock-still, didn't budge, didn't breathe.

Another hard rap on the door. And then, "Paige, are you in there?"

Seth. Tears of joy bathed her eyes, until a niggling fear wiped them away with a glimpse of reality. If Seth came through the door, Eli was in a perfect position to blow him away.

A loud crashing thud lit the air. Paige jumped, heart in her throat. A louder thud sounded, resembling thunder. Hinges whined, and the door rattled.

"Remember, one wrong move and you're dead." Eli's breath spewed hot on her neck as he shoved the handgun deeper into her back. What if she complied? Would he spare her life? Paige swallowed. No more than he planned to spare Seth's. And she needed to do something to prevent that from happening.

Another thundering thud scattered her thoughts. Then the sound of splintering wood echoed through the foyer as the door burst open.

Moving lightning quick, Eli whipped out his weapon and pointed at Seth as his other arm tightened around Paige's neck.

Paige choked and wheezed, her head ready to explode as Seth appeared in the doorway and froze. Gun drawn, face grim, he looked from her to Eli. They were in a stalemate. Nowhere to go. No way to win.

Battling to hold on to her composure, Paige struggled to breathe. She just wanted to beg Seth to turn around and run. He'd sacrificed enough for her, and this time Eli had the upper hand.

Seth sized up the situation in one quick sweep.

Eli was the man. *Crafty. Conniving. A murder.* His gut twisted when he saw Eli with a death grip on Paige. And what bugged him most, he wasn't in a position to do anything about it. At least not yet.

Fear and rage screwed Eli's features. His icy gray stare locked on Seth. "Drop the gun, Garrison." His death grip visibly tightened around Paige's neck.

Paige started to gasp, turn blue. Fear colored her eyes, even as her mouth formed the words *please leave now.*

Rage came on so strong Seth felt ready to burst. "Eli, let Paige go and we'll talk." He kept his voice calm, his gun solidly trained on the man. If he could just buy enough time for help to arrive, they'd have a chance. Maybe.

"Garrison, I have nothing to say except drop the gun

or Paige is dead." Eli flexed his massive arm muscle against Paige's neck; she gasped harder.

Eli's threat arrowed through Seth like lightning. From the crazed look in Eli's eyes, Seth knew he wouldn't hesitate to kill Paige. In fact he was probably looking forward to it. Seth flexed his fingers around his Glock, his mind racing, looking for a way out of this. Not an easy problem to solve.

Eli clearly wasn't in the mood to negotiate, and Seth wasn't about to try anything risky.

"The gun, Garrison." Eli's face contorted, his squinted eyes smoldering.

Jaw clenched, Seth eyed Paige again. Her face pale, the rapid rise and fall of her chest as she struggled to breathe. Fury fueled by fear for her life had him dropping his gun. Then he held up his hands, praying for Eli to let Paige go, let her breathe.

"No, Seth!" Paige's voice came out as a shriek. Eli jumped, his grip loosening, and Paige bolted away from him.

This was Seth's chance. Breaking into a run, he launched himself at Eli, who was frantically wielding his gun, trying to get a clear shot at Paige as she ducked into the next room.

With a scream, Eli slammed into the wall, his gun flying, skittering across the foyer.

"Don't think you're going to win, Garrison!" Eli sprang to his feet, coming at Seth like a charging lion. He threw his first punch, and pain exploded across Seth's lip. He barked a short laugh. "Just wait until I'm through with you."

Seth couldn't wait. In fact, he was planning to make this quick. Curling his fingers tight, Seth went straight for Eli's gut. Eli doubled over and gasped, his eyes bulging. Clearly, the man was better at dishing it out than receiving.

But a second later, he came back, launching his fist in a wild swing. Seth ducked and spun, throwing three punches that connected with Eli's broad jaw. Eli staggered back, rage written on his face. "You've gotten nothing on me, Garrison. I'm just warming up."

Then with a sneer, Eli sent a nail-driving punch into Seth's ribs. Pain rippled across Seth's torso, breath leaving his lungs. He felt droplets of sweat roll down his face as he assumed a fighting stance, teeth clenched.

"Seth! Are you all right?" That was Paige, ready to lunge. Her panicked voice echoed in his ears.

"Stay put," he huffed out as he countered with a fist to Eli's gut, then another solid hit in the jaw, sending Eli staggering back several steps before he straightened again. Then the big brute rushed back at Seth, knocking him to the ground. "Time to get serious, little wimp." He grabbed onto Seth's neck, trying to choke him.

With adrenaline spiking, Seth broke out of Eli's grip and sent an elbow into his rib cage. Struggling to his feet, Seth caught his breath and watched as Eli, several feet away, sluggishly pulled himself up. "I'm not finished with you yet," Eli grunted, punching and kicking mostly at wind.

Too bad, because Seth was finished with him. As Eli lunged for him, Seth threw a front kick, catching Eli in the chest and sending him crashing into the wall. Moaning, Eli tried to come back, regain his footing, but he was hyperventilating. His rapid gasps mingled with the sound of approaching sirens.

Finally. Seth straightened, his face pulsing with pain, muscles burning as police and sheriff's deputies burst into the house.

Paige rushed toward him, her eyes wide. "Seth, are you okay?"

He nodded, his breathing finally under control.

"Thank you for coming here." She took his hand. "And please tell me it's over—really over." The hope in her voice snagged his heart. For once he had a definitive answer for her.

He nodded, squeezing her hand. "Yes, it is. At least for Eli, but I hope a new beginning for us."

Her lips curled into a tentative smile. "For us?" She lifted her hand, running it along his bruised and swollen lip. "Do you mean me and you...together?"

"Yes. Me and you. That is, if you'll have me."

"But what about our past?" Color leached from her face. "I know I've hurt you. I realize now I should have been more understanding—"

"Paige."

She stopped, blinked.

"Let's keep the past in the past. We both made mistakes. I love you and want you with me forever."

"I do... I mean, I will," she whispered, her smile returning. And her smile was like sunshine, the warmth shooting straight to his soul.

Until Paige came back into his life, he'd been stuck in a rut with no plans, no dreams of the future. And now together they had plans, a life together. And this time he promised to never let this blessing God gave him get away.

"I'm so thankful." He smiled, drawing her into his arms. "Because I love you, Paige, and promise to never leave your side again."

Tears filled her eyes. "I love you, too," she whispered as she gazed up at him.

He kissed her then, slowly, earnestly, fingers cupping

her chin while his thumb trailed her jaw. A kiss so sweet, a symbol of hope and love for their new life together.

He couldn't be happier.

"So is this something we need to know about?" Ted stood a short distance away, earning a look from both Seth and Paige. "You guys a couple again?"

Seth exchanged a knowing glance with the woman he loved before he grinned back at Ted. "Yeah. You can say that."

Smiling, his best friend clapped a hand on his shoulder. "Congratulations, you two. So glad you guys finally figured out what the rest of us knew. You were made for each other."

Seth agreed, giving Paige an affectionate squeeze.

EPILOGUE

Six months later

Paige tightened her fingers around her brother's arm. Tears of joy were in her eyes as she stood in the wings, waiting for her big moment to begin.

"Is it okay to cry before the wedding?" Trey chuckled as he rubbed his shoulder up against hers.

Paige took a deep breath. "Happy tears are okay."

"Good. As long as they're happy. I was starting to worry." She smiled at Trey's kidding tone. He was back to his old self. With all charges dropped, he was moving forward and not looking back. She couldn't be happier for him.

The heartwarming instrumental music filling the air started to fade, and a new song began. And with a skip of her heart, she recognized the melody announcing the bride's entrance.

"This is it, little sis." Trey nudged her gently.

She drew a deep breath, so filled with happiness she could barely stand it.

"Ready?"

Buoyed with anticipation, the butterflies inside her flitted freely. She nodded, and they started their walk from the side of the cabin toward the sprawling front lawn set up with rows of white wood folding chairs filled with family and friends.

Her fairy-tale wedding. Her wedding to Seth.

"I'm so happy for you and for Seth. You have a good man." Trey brushed a kiss on her cheek. That meant a lot, coming from him.

"I know," she whispered, nestling close to his side.

The music picked up, and with slow steps they moved toward her groom—who she had to admit looked breathtakingly handsome in his dark tux—standing beside Ted on the top step of the sprawling, now-finished front porch.

Seth smiled as he stepped forward and took her hand. The gleam in his eyes told her all she needed to know. He loved her and she would love him. Forever and ever.

* * * * *

If you liked this story from Annslee Urban,
check out her other Love Inspired Suspense titles:

SMOKY MOUNTAIN INVESTIGATION
BROKEN SILENCE

Available now from Love Inspired!

Find more great reads at www.LoveInspired.com

Dear Reader,

Thank you for reading *Deadly Setup*, my third Love Inspired Suspense book! I hope you enjoyed getting to know Seth and Paige as they worked through issues in their lives to restore the broken trust and love they once shared.

I love writing about strong men and women who can move past the hurt and rejection in their lives, learning to trust and love again while looking to God to guide them. One thing I've learned in my life is the need to forgive freely, forget the past and love unconditionally. I hope my characters serve to encourage others to do the same. Not that it's an easy task. As for me, I'm still a work in progress.

I love hearing from readers. You can contact me at maryannsleeurban@gmail.com or find me on Facebook as Annslee Urban or www.facebook.com/mary.a.urban.9.

I can *do all things* through Christ who strengthens me. Philippians 4:13 NKJV.

Blessings and beyond!
Annslee Urban

SPECIAL EXCERPT FROM

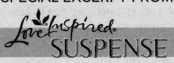

When former navy nurse Stella Silverstone returns to her hometown to care for her grandmother, someone wants her out of the way—preferably dead. But Chance Miller, owner of the security and rescue agency where she works, will put his own life on the line to guard her.

Read on for a sneak preview of
THE CHRISTMAS TARGET by Shirlee McCoy,
available November 2016 from Love Inspired Suspense!

"I need to keep Beatrice safe," Stella murmured, trying to refocus her thoughts, keep them where they needed to be. "The guy who attacked me is still out there, and I can't count on him not returning."

Chance heard the worry in Stella's voice, and the weariness. She wasn't asking for help, but they both knew she needed it.

"We'll keep her safe."

We'll keep you safe, too was on the tip of his tongue, but he didn't say it. Stella prided herself on being able to handle just about anything. She didn't like needing help, but she'd take it when necessary. This was one of the few times when it absolutely was.

"I appreciate that, Chance, but Cooper and his department—"

"Aren't going to be able to provide twenty-four-hour protection. HEART can."

LISEXP1016

"At what cost? Another job? A client who really needs your help not getting it because you're here helping me?"

"We have plenty of manpower, Stella, and you know it. If you don't want us here, you'll have to come up with a better reason than that." She wouldn't. Because she knew HEART could do what needed to be done faster and better than just about anyone else.

She shrugged.

"If you want HEART out, say so," he prodded, and she sighed.

"I would, but I do need the help. Much as I hate to admit it, my brain isn't functioning at a fast enough pace to keep my grandmother safe."

Whomever the attacker was, he had motive, he had means and he wasn't messing around. Two attempts in a few hours meant he was also desperate.

For what?

That was the question Chance needed to answer.

If he did, he'd have the answer to everything else.

Except what he was going to do once Stella was safe and there was nothing standing between them but her reluctance to be hurt and his decision to let her walk away.

Don't miss
THE CHRISTMAS TARGET by Shirlee McCoy,
available November 2016 wherever
Love Inspired® Suspense books and ebooks are sold.

www.LoveInspired.com

LISEXP1016